Dealing with an ex-best friend, a new *girl* best friend, and a
heartbreaking hamster, David Greenberg is learning . . .

How to
Survive
Middle School

Also by Donna Gephart

As If Being 12¾ Isn't Bad Enough,
My Mother Is Running for President!

Olivia Bean, Trivia Queen
AVAILABLE FROM DELACORTE PRESS IN SPRING 2012

Dealing with an ex-best friend, a new *girl* best friend, and a
heartbreaking hamster, David Greenberg is learning . . .

How to
Survive
Middle School

Donna Gephart

A Yearling Book

Text copyright © 2010 by Donna Gephart
Cover photograph copyright © 2010 by Getty Images

All rights reserved. Published in the United States by Yearling, an imprint of Random House Children's Books, a division of Random House, Inc., New York. Originally published in hardcover in the United States by Delacorte Press, an imprint of Random House Children's Books, New York, in 2010.

Yearling and the jumping horse design are registered trademarks of Random House, Inc.

Visit us on the Web! www.randomhouse.com/kids

Educators and librarians, for a variety of teaching tools, visit us at
www.randomhouse.com/teachers

The Library of Congress has cataloged the hardcover edition of this work as follows:
Gephart, Donna.
How to survive middle school / Donna Gephart. — 1st ed.
p. cm.
Summary: When thirteen-year-old David Greenberg's best friend makes the start of middle school even worse than he feared it could be, David becomes friends with Sophie, who shares his love of television shows and posts one of their skits on YouTube, making them wildly popular—online, at least.
ISBN 978-0-385-73793-7 (hc) — ISBN 978-0-385-90701-9 (lib. bdg.) —
ISBN 978-0-375-89587-6 (ebook)
[1. Middle schools—Fiction. 2. Schools—Fiction. 3. Best friends—Fiction.
4. Friendship—Fiction. 5. Popularity—Fiction. 6. Video recordings—Production and direction—Fiction. 7. YouTube (Electronic resource)—Fiction.]
I. Title.
PZ7.G293463How 2010
[Fic]—dc22
2009021809

ISBN 978-0-375-85411-8 (pbk.)

Printed in the United States of America

20 19 18 17 16 15 14 13 12 11

First Yearling Edition 2011

To Dan, Andrew and Jake, with love

ACKNOWLEDGMENTS

Thanks to Tina Wexler for being both an excellent agent and a wonderful friend.

My stories are always in good hands when they're in the hands of my editor, Stephanie Elliott. Stephanie invests much time and heart into finding what belongs in a story and what doesn't. It's a privilege to work with her and her assistant, Krista Vitola.

I'm grateful to the talented people at Random House for endless encouragement and support during every step of the publishing process.

Middle-school media specialist Lisa Petroccia, who is a master at creating video projects with the students, assisted with my research.

Thanks to the WIMS news team for allowing me to watch them in action, especially Paola for teaching me about the equipment.

Lawrence Schimel and Caren Wilder helped with a Spanish translation. ¡*Gracias!*

Caren also gave me the Jewish apple cake recipe many years ago, never imagining it would end up in a book.

Elysa Graber-Lipperman and her lovely daughter, Amelia, read an early draft and provided useful feedback.

Much appreciation to Riley Roam and Kenny Mikey from Page Turner Adventures (www.pageturneradventures.com) for their excellent work on the videos and for their valued friendship.

Love and gratitude to my Sunday writing group— Sensational Sylvia, Lovely Linda, Debonair Dan, Jazzy Jill, Capable Carole, Knowledgeable Kieran and Positively Peter— for laughing in all the right places.

The first day of summer vacation is important, because what you do that day sets the tone for the rest of summer.

That's why my best friend, Elliott Berger, is coming over to watch the *Daily Show* episodes I've recorded. Mom and I used to watch them together. She always said the host, Jon Stewart, stood up for the little guy, which is funny, because Jon Stewart *is* a little guy—five feet seven inches. According to Wikipedia, the average height for men in the United States is five feet nine and a half inches.

Let's just say I can totally relate to Jon's height issue.

Anyway, I record other shows, like *The Colbert Report* and *Late Show*, too, but mostly Elliott and I watch *The Daily Show*. We both think Jon Stewart is hilarious and a great interviewer. Someday I'm going to be a famous talk show host like Jon.

He and I have a lot in common.

1. We're both Jewish.

2. We both have our own talk shows—but mine's different from his. It's called *TalkTime* and I post the shows on YouTube.

3. We're both vertically challenged (but I still have time to grow).

Since Elliott won't be here for a while, I shoot my first *TalkTime* of the summer without him.

First I set up the studio (aka my bedroom) by taping a poster of New York City's skyline on my wall, kind of like they do on the *Late Show with David Letterman*. That way it looks like I'm shooting in an exciting location instead of boring Bensalem, Pennsylvania, where the biggest news is that they opened a Golden Corral buffet restaurant on Street Road. (Yes, I know that's a weird name for a road, but that's what it's called. It's almost as stupid as parking in a driveway and driving on a parkway.)

Anyway, next I make sure my special guest is ready in the greenroom (aka the bathroom).

He is.

Finally, I set my camera on the tripod in my bedroom, bang two empty paper-towel rolls together and say, "Action!"

Using my best talk show host voice, I begin: "Welcome to *TalkTime* with David Greenberg." I scribble on a piece of paper with a grand flourish, like Jon Stewart does on *The Daily Show*. Then I crumple the paper, toss it into my laundry basket and keep talking. "It's our first show of the summer and it's going to be a hot one. Ha! Ha!"

I hear Hammy's wheel spin like crazy, so I turn the camera toward his cage and give him a close-up. "And now," I say, "your moment of Hammy." As though on cue, Hammy hops off his wheel, looks up and twitches his whiskers.

I smile and think about how I'll edit that later, showing a split screen—Hammy on the right, credits scrolling on the left.

I point the camera back at myself and sit in front of fake New York. "Before we get to today's special guest, it's time for Top Six and a Half with David Greenberg.

"Top Six and a Half Things That I, David Todd Greenberg, Will Miss About Longwood Elementary School.

"One: The lunch lady who snuck ice cream onto my tray every Friday. By the way, awesome hairnet, lunch lady.

"Two: Student of the Week, which I won a total of seven times—more than anyone in the history of Longwood El. Wahoo!"

I pace around my room until I come up with number three. "Three: Helping Ms. Florez in the TV studio with morning announcements. She said I was the best news anchor she ever had."

I pace again and trip on the tripod. The camera topples, but I catch it. I can edit that out later, though it'll make a weird jump in the action. It would probably be safer if I wrote my Top Six and a Half before I filmed them!

Back in front of fake New York, I take a deep breath and say, "Four: Spanish Club.

"Five: Academic Games.

"Six: Watching Coach Lukasik, who is definitely not vertically challenged—that man could be an NBA superstar—hula hoop during P.E. with the girls.

"And the thing I'll miss most about Longwood El?

"Six and one-half: *Everything!*"

I turn off the camera and flop onto my bed. I wish Longwood El didn't stop after fifth grade. When my sister, Lindsay, who's fourteen now, went there, it went through sixth. That was before the overcrowding problem.

Now sixth grade is at Harman Middle School. I've heard rumors about Harman—Harm Man!—but they're probably just meant to scare incoming sixth graders. Lindsay graduated from Harman and she's fine. I mean, except for her face, which is almost always covered with zits.

Middle school, I'm sure, will be great.

I turn the camera on again and sit tall. "Now it's time for our special guest. And he happens to be none other than the ultra-famous . . . Oh, wait a second, he's still in the greenroom. Let's surprise him."

I grab my camera from the tripod and walk along the hallway, then I kick open the bathroom door. Inside, I zoom in on the cover of the *Entertainment Weekly* lying on the toilet lid and say, "Our guest today is the veeeery famous talk show host Jon Stewart." I remind myself to add applause later when I edit the show on my computer. I hold the magazine to get a good shot of Jon's photo, his trademark goofy grin beaming up from the cover.

I imagine *my* picture on the cover of *Entertainment Weekly* . . . someday. If Mom ever saw me on a magazine cover in a store, she'd probably borrow a stranger's cell phone right then and there and call me, screaming with excitement. I grin, just like Jon Stewart.

Someday.

But for now, I put the camera on the bathroom counter, point it toward myself and kneel so I'm lined up with it. This isn't easy. I should probably wait until Elliott's here to shoot this part so he can hold the camera, or I should at least get my tripod, but I'm on a roll, so I keep going.

"Is it true you played the French horn in the school band?" I ask Magazine Cover Jon. I know it's true, because I looked it up, and I think it's interesting because my mom plays the tuba. *Played* the tuba. Now her tuba still sits in our living room, even though nobody's touched it for two years.

I hold Magazine Cover Jon in front of the camera and speak as though I'm him. This is tough, because though I'm a guy, my voice hasn't quite caught on yet. "That's right, David," Magazine Cover Jon says. "For your viewers who don't know what the French horn is, it's a large, shiny girl repellent."

I laugh, even though I made up the joke. "I know what you mean," I say, but somewhere between "what" and "you" my voice squeaks. Dad says my vocal cords are lengthening and I'm transitioning from boy to man. I say that if my body were a door, my voice would be its rusty hinge. I wonder if Elliott's voice still cracks. Probably not. His vocal cords must be done lengthening, just like the rest of him; he's at least three inches taller than me.

I rerecord that part, then say to Magazine Cover Jon, "I'm going to be a famous talk show host one day."

Magazine Cover Jon is ultraexcited by this news. "Is that so?" he asks, "his" voice cracking on the last word. I keep going.

"Yes," I tell him. "When I go to middle school, I hope they have a TV studio so I can—"

Behind me, I hear the bathroom door open and hit the wall. I whirl around and train the camera on Lindsay's scrunched-up, squinty-eyed face.

"What the heck are you doing, David? Don't you know what time it is?" Lindsay's got gunk plastered in spots all over her skin—zit-be-gone stuff that will probably work as well as all the other zit-be-gone stuff she's used, meaning not at all.

Zits are a part of puberty I'm not looking forward to. That and hair sprouting in weird places and stinky armpits (which are starting already). According to *Ripley's Believe It or Not*, there are 516,000 smelly bacteria per square inch in an armpit.

Lindsay puts her hands on her hips. "Do you realize it's seven o'clock in the morning?"

I check my watch. "Seven-oh-five, actually."

"Whatever!" she says as a crusty piece of gunk falls from her face and lands on the bathroom floor. "It's the first day of summer, David, in case you didn't notice. And I'd like to sleep, oh, later than seven-oh-five."

I check my watch again. "Seven-oh-six."

Even with gunk on them, Lindsay's cheeks redden. This is not a good sign. Sometimes when her cheeks get red, she throws things. At me!

"David," Lindsay says, "just go back to your room and be quiet."

My sister taps the cover of *Entertainment Weekly* with her pink-polished fingernail, inadvertently poking my special guest in the eye. "What the heck are you doing in here, anyway?"

I pull my scrawny shoulders back and tell her the first thing that pops into my mind: "I'm going to be a famous talk show host. See?" I shove the magazine's cover in her face.

Lindsay squints at the magazine, then at me. "Jon Stewart. Hmmm. Jewish. Short. Yeah, I can see it."

I remember one of my favorite segments from my *TalkTime* show. "Hey, Lindsay?"

When she focuses on me, I turn on the camera and get a close-up of her zit-cream-covered face.

"David!" She hides her face with her hands, pivots and storms down the hall. Her door slams loudly enough that I hope it doesn't wake Dad. The last thing I need is another uninvited guest barging into the greenroom.

I close the bathroom door and think of the words I'll print under Lindsay's face when I edit the video: *Today's acne forecast: cloudy with a chance of blackheads.*

The moment I finish my interview, there's pounding on the door. "Come on, David," Dad says. "Hurry it up."

We live in an old house with only one bathroom for the entire upstairs. Sharing it becomes a pain, especially when Lindsay does her zits-be-gone routine. I'm grateful Bubbe has her own apartment downstairs with its own bathroom or she'd probably barge in on me, too.

"Coming!" I turn off the camera and flush. No need to let Dad know I was making a video in our bathroom.

When I open the door, Dad runs a hand through his scary morning hair and belches. " 'Scuse me."

"Sure," I say, a little grossed out, and walk past him with the magazine and the camera behind my back.

In my room, I put the camera on my desk, plop onto my bed, stare at Hammy running like a maniac on his wheel and think, *Jon Stewart, I'll bet you didn't start out this way!*

2

Before Elliott arrives, I edit my *TalkTime* video and upload it to YouTube.

Without Elliott helping, the credits read *Director—David Greenberg; Producer—David Greenberg; Cameraman—David Greenberg; Host—David Greenberg; Special Guest Star—Magazine Cover Jon Stewart; Daily Acne Forecast—Lindsay Greenberg; World-Famous Hamster—Hammy Greenberg.*

I think this is one of my best videos yet. Too bad the only people who watch them and comment are Elliott, Bubbe, Ms. Florez from Longwood El and someone named LADM. I wish I could e-mail Mom and tell her about this new one. But I can't. And even if I could, she wouldn't be able to watch it anyway. I'm sure she'll catch up to the twenty-first century. Someday.

By the time Elliott finally shows—late, as usual—I have everything ready for the perfect first day of summer. Paul Newman's popcorn is in a bowl on the coffee table in the living room.

And my red plastic tub of K'nex building pieces sits near Mom's tuba in the corner for after we're done watching the *Daily Show* episodes.

When I open the door for Elliott, he walks into the living room, drops his yearbook on the coffee table and asks, "What do you think this means?"

"Hey, Elliott. Nice to see you, too."

"This is serious, David. I looked through my yearbook, and Cara Epstein put not one but two hearts after her name. See?" He points to two tiny purple hearts. "What do you think this means?"

I consider telling Elliott it means he's crazy, but one look at his face lets me know this would be cruel, so I study the writing as though it's a newly discovered bit of hieroglyphics.

Elliott, have a great summer. Good luck in sixth grade. Cara

The purple hearts appear after her name. The same purple hearts she drew after her signature in *my* yearbook. But something about Elliott—maybe his wild eyes, or the way he looks like I might be about to say he has three weeks left to live—tells me that now is not the right time to be honest. So I shut his yearbook, take a deep breath as though I'm about to spout some deep, ancient wisdom and say, "No clue."

"No clue!" Elliott paces our living room. "You're supposed to be my friend."

"I am your friend, moron!" I shove Elliott's shoulder.

"Then help me, supermoron!" He shoves back. "I've been obsessing about this since yesterday." Elliott stares into my eyes. "Do you think Cara Epstein likes me?"

"Do I think Cara Epstein likes you?" It's at this moment I look at Elliott, really look at him, and notice he has the beginnings of a mustache over either side of his upper lip. I guess I'd always thought it was a shadow or chocolate milk or dirt, but standing this close to him, I can tell it's the fine dark hairs of an actual mustache.

I feel like somebody punched me in the gut. My upper lip is as hairless as Paul Shaffer's bald head.

"What do you think?" Elliott gulps a handful of popcorn. "Does she like me?"

My breathing accelerates. Elliott is turning into a man-boy. And I'm still a scrawny, clear-skinned, no-hint-of-a-muscle-anywhere-on-my-body boy-boy.

"David?"

There is desperation in Elliott's eyes. I haven't seen him look this intense since he found a rare Charizard card in a new pack of Pokémon trading cards in first grade.

"David!" he shrieks.

"What's going on?" Dad shouts from his office on the other side of the house.

"Nothing!" I yell. "Sorry, Dad!" I punch Elliott hard in the arm. "Shut up."

"Ow," Elliott says, rubbing his arm. "I forgot your dad's working, but I'm going crazy here."

"Shhh," I say, afraid Elliott will scream again. I look at the entry in Elliott's yearbook, then at Elliott. At the entry. At Elliott. Entry. Elliott. I know there's only one thing I can say to calm him. "Yes, I definitely think Cara Epstein likes you."

His eyes look like they're going to burst out of their sockets. *Does he expect me to say something else?*

"A lot."

Elliott practically lunges at me. "What makes you say that?"

"The, um, hearts. If she liked you a little, she'd have put one heart, but she put two."

"Then why didn't she put three?" Elliott is actually sweating. Over Cara Epstein, who is this ordinary girl who threw up once in second grade after eating expired strawberry yogurt.

"David!"

"Overkill. Three would have been overkill." I feel like I'm talking him down from a ledge. If this is what liking a girl does to you, I want no part of it until I'm at least thirty.

"You're right." Elliott relaxes next to me on the couch. "This is good. Very good."

"Elliott?"

He looks distracted. "Yeah?"

"Can we watch *The Daily Show* now?"

He pats his yearbook. "Yeah, totally. Put it on." He grabs another handful of popcorn. "Let the marathon begin."

I lean back, feeling like I just performed an exorcism. After starting the show, I grab some popcorn and think about what a great first day of summer this is going to be.

But during Jon Stewart's opening monologue, I catch Elliott peeking at his yearbook. I want to hurl it across the room and tell him to pay attention.

At the first commercial, Elliott opens his yearbook again, and my heart sinks. "Hey, David, want to go to the mall?"

I look at the TV and at the K'nex box in the corner and at El-liott. "Why? There's nothing fun to do at the mall, except the food court."

"I know." Elliott's cheeks grow red. "But Cara might be hang-ing out there."

"We've got *The Daily Shows* to watch and K'nex for later." *The perfect summer day.*

"Yeah, but don't you think the mall might be fun, too?"

I feel my perfect day slipping away.

"No, I'd rather—"

"I'll owe you big," Elliott says.

I remind myself how many years we've been friends, except for that time in first grade when we didn't talk for two weeks be-cause he said Batman was way better than Superman. Any idiot knows that aside from his little Kryptonite issue, Superman is far superior.

"Sure," I say, switching off the TV. "Daaad! Can you drive us to the mall?"

"David," Elliott says, shoving my shoulder, "this is going to be the best summer ever."

"Totally," I say, though the way things are going, I have my doubts. "Daaaaaaad!"

"Yeah, I'll drive you," Dad calls from his office. "Give me a minute."

"All right!" Elliott punches me in the arm. "This is so great."

My arm hurts where he punched me. *Yeah, so great.*

3

I was right about the first day setting the tone for the entire summer.

Now it's September, and Elliott and I have gone to the mall a total of twenty-four times. Twenty-four! That's more than Lindsay and her girlfriends have gone. And they're *girls*!

I can't believe I've spent my entire summer cruising past Victoria's Secret with Elliott. He says he thinks Cara might shop in there. Yeah, right! He likes looking at the underwear on the mannequins. *Get a catalog, perv!*

Every time we've walked past, I hoped Elliott would come to his senses and want to do something fun. This was no way for a guy to spend his *entire* summer.

But Elliott never caught on that this was incredibly boring. To make things worse, we saw Cara Epstein a grand total of once. She was sitting at the fountain with Ethan Leikach, Elyssa Silverman and Jared Stevens. Elliott didn't even have the guts to walk up and say hi.

On the last Friday of summer break, I sip a Mango Madness shake at the food court and shoot mental darts at a little scar on Elliott's forehead. "We didn't make one video together all summer," I mumble.

"Huh?" Elliott asks, putting down the iced coffee I bought for him.

"Nothing," I say.

"What's wrong?" he asks.

Everything. "Nothing."

"Good," Elliott says.

"Good."

Elliott goes back to acting like he's so grown-up, drinking coffee and checking out the girls walking by.

I go back to shooting mental darts at his forehead.

We had so much fun together last summer. We built swords and shields out of empty paper-towel rolls, cereal boxes and silver foil and had superhero battles in my driveway. Once, we built a giant K'nex Ferris wheel and roller coaster that actually worked. Elliott's not allowed to have friends over when his mom's at work. And since his dad walked out on them, she's always at work. That was why Elliott practically lived at our house, and we had such great times together.

What happened to all that fun? What happened to *Elliott?* All he wants to do now is talk about girls. More specifically, about whether Cara Epstein likes him. A few times, I considered telling Elliott I thought Cara drew two purple hearts in everyone's yearbook, but I couldn't do that to him. Even though he did ruin my summer.

Well, at least there's still Labor Day weekend. And Elliott promised to help make our best *TalkTime* video ever.

I kick him under the table.

"Wha?" He bends and rubs his leg.

"You're helping me shoot on Monday. Right?"

"Yeah. Whatever."

"Really," I say, trying to find a glimmer of my old friend. "Are you going to be there or what? We haven't made one video the whole summer and school starts Tuesday."

He glares at me. "I said I'll be there."

"Good. Shooting starts at nine. Be on time."

"I *said* I'll be there."

I take a long, loud slurp of Mango Madness.

When Elliott looks up, annoyed, I'm glad.

"My aunt's pool party is tomorrow," I say.

"Have fun," he says in a way that means the opposite.

"I will," I say. But I know I won't. My cousin Jack will be there, and he terrifies me. Last year, I accidentally fell into their swimming pool, fully dressed and holding a paper plate piled with potato salad. And I can't swim! Especially through chunks of potato salad.

"Good for you," Elliott says.

"Good for you," I mock. Then I lean close and say, "You know, it's not my fault Cara only showed once at the mall." *And you didn't have the guts to talk to her.*

Elliott makes a face like he swallowed an ice cube. "Shut up!"

I chuck my empty cup at him and start walking.

"Hey," Elliott says. "Where you going?"

I turn around and yell as loudly as I can, "Out of this stupid mall!"

"Wait up." Elliott runs after me.

I don't stop until I'm outside at the bench where Dad is supposed to pick us up. I expect Elliott to say he's sorry, but he just stands next to me, rocking back on his heels.

When Dad finally pulls up, I get into the front seat, leaving Elliott to climb into the back by himself.

"Thanks for the ride, Mr. Greenberg," Elliott says.

"No problem. You guys have a good time?"

"Great," I say, hoping to end the conversation.

"Yeah," Elliott says, kicking the back of my seat. "Great."

When Dad stops in front of Elliott's apartment building, Elliott and I barely nod at each other. I watch him disappear inside the building and my stomach tightens.

I want to tell Dad that Elliott's been acting like a total idiot this summer. But Dad is humming and tapping the steering wheel, and ever since Mom left, it's rare to see him this happy, so I don't say anything to ruin his mood.

As we drive away, I squint at Elliott's living room window. He's waving.

I wave back, but I'm sure our car is too far gone for Elliott to see.

4

It's blistering hot by eleven a.m. I've applied SPF 45 sunscreen three times to every exposed area of flesh, which isn't much, since I'm wearing long swim trunks and a T-shirt.

Lindsay and our cousin Amy, who is one year older than Lindsay, have staked out lounge chairs near the edge of the pool. They've slathered themselves with baby oil—*baby oil!*—hoping to attract sun to their skin. And they've already turned an angry shade of pink. Are they insane? Haven't they ever heard of melanoma? Basal cell carcinoma? Squamous cell carcinoma? I should make a public service announcement about it when Elliott and I shoot our video Monday.

"Hey, Lindsay?" I say.

"Yeah?" She doesn't bother lifting her eyelids.

"If olive oil comes from olives, and vegetable oil comes from vegetables, where does baby oil come from?"

"You're gross!" Amy says, and chucks the baby oil bottle at me.

Luckily, I scoot out of the way, but she makes me pick up the bottle and bring it back.

I pace near the pool's edge, deciding if I want to go in the shallow end to cool off.

"Don't slip, David," Amy yells from her lounge chair. "You know what happened last year."

Lindsay, Amy and our other cousin Rachel, who's six and is paddling around the pool on her dinosaur float, crack up.

"Ha-ha." I wish I were home with Hammy, shooting a *TalkTime* video. In air-conditioning.

A shadow falls over me, blocking the sun. *Thank goodness!* I turn and look up, expecting to see a fluffy cloud. Instead, I see Cousin Jack. He's grown at least six inches since last summer and wastes no time getting me into a killer vise-grip headlock. My nice clean head is millimeters away from Jack's hairy armpit and about 516,000 bacteria per square inch!

While crushing my neck with his muscular arm, Jack walks me past Lindsay and Amy. They don't even look up. He drags me past the gate to where Dad, Bubbe and Aunt Sherry lie in shade on lounge chairs. All the while, Jack gives me noogies and smacks my head in a supposedly friendly way.

"David and I are hanging out for a while," Jack says.

"Have a good time, boys," Dad says, raising his beer bottle, as though seeing his only son in a headlock is cause for celebration.

"Have fun," Aunt Sherry calls, not putting down her *People* magazine.

"Don't do anything stupid, Jack," Bubbe yells. "And for goodness' sake, let go of your cousin. You'll bruise his neck. Sherry, are you watching your son?"

Aunt Sherry waves a perfectly manicured hand to show she heard Bubbe, but doesn't lift her gaze from the magazine. "Have fun, guys."

Bubbe huffs and crosses her arms over her floral-print bathing suit.

Jack drags me through the house and out the front door.

I make lame gurgling sounds and wonder if I'll have to wear a neck brace to school Tuesday.

When we're out front, next to Aunt Sherry's Volvo, Jack removes his sweaty arm. I turn my neck in each direction to make sure nothing is broken, then take my first deep breath in a while.

"Hey," I say.

"Hey, little man," Jack says, hoisting himself onto the Volvo's roof, his legs dangling over the rear window. It takes a couple of attempts before I'm able to drag myself up.

Jack whacks me on the back. "So . . ."

"So," I say, hoping to get that perfect mixture of laid-back and cool, but my voice cracks and I manage to achieve two totally different girly sounds in one lousy syllable.

"Congrats on getting out of that baby school," Jack says. "Must be a relief."

I nod, thinking that's the right response.

Jack pulls a lighter and a pack of cigarettes from the pocket inside his swim trunks. I'm scared he's going to make me smoke, but he just puts a cigarette between his lips and lights up. He turns his head away and exhales grayish white smoke.

Jack squints. "Ready for Hormone Middle?"

"Harman?" I ask, thinking that Jack mispronounced the name

of the school. Bubbe says Jack's elevator doesn't go all the way up to the penthouse. "*Harman* Middle School, right?"

Jack laughs and starts coughing. "Yeah, yeah. Harman. Isn't that what I said?"

No.

"I'm telling you, little man . . . it's a pit there."

Maybe Harman was bad for you because you're bad, I think. *I'm sure Elliott and I are going to love it . . . if he ever stops obsessing about Cara Epstein.*

Jack gets this serious look on his face that actually scares me. "You gotta watch out, David."

"Watch out?" My throat goes burnt-bagel dry. I swallow repeatedly, but it doesn't help. "Jack, I need to go inside and get a drink."

He pats my thigh. "In a minute, little man. We're still talking."

The backs of my legs are melting. I don't want to talk to Jack about this. Jack blows smoke and flicks his stubby, still-lit cigarette into the street. "If you don't watch out, you'll . . ." He looks down and shakes his head.

"I'll what?" My heart hammers before I remember that Lindsay went to Harman and didn't have problems. Then I get it. Jack's trying to scare me. I play along. "I'll bet there are monsters in the boys' bathroom. Right?"

"I'm not kidding." Jack looks right into my eyes, and I smell cigarette smoke on his breath. "I'm trying to help you here."

"I didn't mean—"

"No monsters," Jack says, lighting another cigarette. "But

don't use the sinks in the boys' bathroom. Guys pee in them when they're in a hurry and the urinals are taken."

"No way." *How will I wash my hands?*

"Yeah way." Jack pokes me in the chest.

At Longwood El, Ms. Bonino, the principal, hugged the students when they walked in each morning. Even fifth graders. And most of them hugged back.

"And there are always fights at Hormone. When a fight breaks out, it's okay to watch as long as you don't get in the way. Or, if there's a fight in the hallway and it's your lunch period, run to the cafeteria. Everyone will be watching the fight, so there won't be a line." Jack nods.

I nod, too. It seems like the right thing to do, but inside, my heart takes off like Hammy running full tilt on his wheel. When our fifth-grade class toured Harman, there was a policewoman in the cafeteria. I thought that was scary at the time. While we were there, she broke up a fight between two girls. *Girls!* One of the girls pulled the other's hair, and that girl yelled something I'm not allowed to say. The next thing I knew, the policewoman ran over and got kicked in the stomach during the scuffle. I thought that was *really* scary.

Our tour guide—the cheerleading coach at Harman—rushed us out of the cafeteria toward the science wing. I got so excited about the cool microscopes and lab equipment that it took my mind off the incident. I haven't given it much thought since then. Until now.

"If you don't want to get in a fight," Jack says, blowing smoke, "don't get on anybody's bad side."

"I won't," I say, meaning it, because I, David Todd Greenberg, do not fight.

"Also," Jack says, "don't stand around after school in the courtyard, 'cause that's where the bad kids hang." He lights another cigarette. "I should know." He laughs at his own joke.

I laugh, too, but it's a nervous, I-don't-want-to-die-in-middle-school kind of laugh. "But you got through okay." I look at Jack, hoping for encouragement.

"Sure. Sure," he says. "But even for a guy like me"—he touches his chest—"sixth grade stunk." Jack looks me up and down and flicks me in the stomach. "You should bulk up, little man. Lift weights. Do push-ups. *Something!* And whatever you do . . ." Jack's so close I have to keep from gagging on cigarette odor. "Stay away from the bathrooms around your birthday, especially the one on the second floor near the science wing."

I wipe sweat from my hairless upper lip. "Why?"

Jack reels back. "You haven't heard? Come on."

I shake my head.

"Everyone knows."

My throat constricts.

"On your birthday, eighth graders drag you into the bathroom, then shove your head into the toilet and flush while making you sing 'Happy Birthday.' You know, a swirlie."

"No!"

"Yeah. I'm telling you so you can look out for yourself, David. If I still went there—if I flunked or something—I'd totally look out for you, but I won't be there."

"Yeah, thanks." I feel dazed, light-headed.

"Your sister won't be there, either, so you're gonna have to take care of yourself." He punches me in the arm and it really hurts, but I don't rub it. "A guy like you has to watch out."

A guy like me? "Well, um, thanks for the advice." My hands tremble. "I'd better get back."

"One more thing," Jack says. "There's a kid named Tommy Murphy."

"I know Tommy Murphy," I say. "He lives in Elliott's apartment building."

"That kid's crazy mean," Jack says. "Stay away from him."

"I will," I say. "He once threw a rock at Elliott's forehead and split it wide open."

"I believe it," Jack says. "Once at Harman, he flipped a kid over the railing. An ambulance had to come and everything."

"Was the kid okay?"

Jack shrugs. "I heard he broke three ribs and fractured his skull."

Sweat drips from every pore on my body. "No."

"Yeah. Just stay away from him and from that bathroom on the second floor near the science wing."

My stomach coils into a tight knot. Before Jack can even flick away his cigarette, I slide off the car, burn the backs of my legs even more and limp into Aunt Sherry's house. I drag myself through the house to the backyard and stumble to the pool area, hoping Lindsay is still there.

She is, on her lounge chair—a giant bull's-eye for the sun's cancer-causing rays. But that's not important now.

I kneel beside Lindsay and tap her warm shoulder. I know that even though I irritate her on a daily basis, she'll tell me the truth. She always tells me the truth. "Um, Linds?"

"You mind?" she says, brushing off her shoulder where I tapped her. "I'm tanning here and you're blocking the sun."

Amy raises one eyelid, looks at me, sighs and closes it again.

"One question, Lindsay. Please." I nudge her shoulder. "It's important."

Lindsay's eyelids open, and she leans on one elbow as though it's incredibly strenuous. "Make it quick." She sniffs. "David! Were you smoking?"

I tilt my head and look at her.

"Probably Jack's," Amy says.

"Oh, right," Lindsay says, then focuses on me. "What's your question?"

"You went to Harman, right?"

Lindsay swipes at her forehead. "You *know* I went to Harman, David. That was one question. You're done." She flops back on the lounge chair and closes her eyelids again.

"Lindsay, please."

"Whaaaaat?"

I take a deep breath and whisper, "On your birthday, do eighth graders drag you into the bathroom and make you sing while they flush your head?" I'm positive she's going to laugh and say I'm an idiot. At least, I hope she does.

Lindsay laughs.

I sigh. Jack wasn't trying to warn me; he was trying to scare me. *Jerk!*

"I'd forgotten about that," Lindsay says. "When I was in seventh, they did that to Trevor Johnson, a sixth grader, on his birthday. Remember?" She pokes Amy's arm.

Amy nods without opening her eyelids. "Yeah, I heard about that."

Lindsay continues. "He came to P.E. dripping. Dripping! Coach Shank wouldn't let Trevor go to the nurse or anything. He made him take a shower and dress out for P.E. It was sooooo funny."

Funny? My stomach squeezes. "What happened to him?"

Lindsay waves her hand. "I heard he transferred to another school or something."

"Oh," I say, as though it's no big deal. But it *is* a big deal. I can't have my head flushed. I may never recover from the psychological trauma. What if some weird bacteria from the water travels up my nose and infects my brain and I die a slow, horrible death?

Despite the blazing sun, I must look paler than usual, because Lindsay says, "Don't worry, David. It's not like they do that to *every* sixth grader." She pats my knee. "Just the really weird ones."

"Oh, great." Questions swirl around my mind. *Is the toilet full of you-know-what? How long do they hold your head down? Can a person actually drown in a toilet bowl?* The drowning-prevention expert who came to our school said a person can drown in a couple of inches of water. A couple of inches!

"Really, David, you have nothing to worry about."

"No?"

"No," Lindsay says. "Your birthday's during winter break. You won't even be in school then."

"But Jack said—"

"I'm telling you, David—there's nothing to panic about."

I'm panicked.

"Now get out. You're blocking the sun." And Lindsay shoves me. Not hard or anything, but I'm so shaky from what Jack told me that I stumble backward.

As I fall, I windmill my arms as though it will do anything other than make me look like an idiot. Every panicked thought flies from my mind except one: *Please, God. Not again.*

I smack the pool's surface and sink in the lukewarm water. For a terrifying moment, I think I'm drowning in a giant toilet bowl.

But I can't be drowning, because my head's already out of the water and I'm holding on to the edge and looking at my cousin Rachel, who's clutching her dinosaur float and spluttering.

I can tell by her squinty eyes she's pissed.

I bumped into something when I fell into the pool. Must've been her.

"David!" Rachel says, squeezing the dinosaur's inflatable neck with one hand and pinching my arm hard with the other. "Stop. Falling. Into. Our. Pool!"

"It's not like I . . . At least I wasn't holding potato . . . oh . . ." My arms tremble as I hoist myself out. I'm coughing and dripping and surprised Dad isn't standing beside the pool to make sure I'm okay. I squint toward the back of the house. Of course Dad's not standing beside the pool. He's lying on his lounge chair, beer in hand.

Amy and Lindsay laugh as though the sight of me, nearly drowned, is hilarious. Even Rachel laughs and makes faces.

Well, at least I'm not thirsty anymore. I swallowed tons of chlorinated pool water.

"It's like an annual tradition," Amy says.

Shielding her eyes from the sun, Lindsay asks, "You all right, David?"

I don't answer. I walk away from them, toward the house.

Dad gives me a strange look as I pass.

"Oh, Davey," Bubbe says, pressing her palms to her cheeks.

Aunt Sherry laughs and shakes her head. "Not again, sweetie." She points toward the house. "Towels in the guest bathroom."

I ignore everyone and walk to the guest bathroom, not even caring that I'm dripping water all over Aunt Sherry's carpets and floors. Does she think I have the IQ of a Twinkie? I know there are towels in the guest bathroom. It's a bathroom.

While I'm drying off, I glance at the toilet and feel my chest tighten.

If I, David Todd Greenberg, can't survive my aunt's stupid pool party without nearly drowning, how am I going to survive middle school?

6

Late Sunday morning, Dad walks into my room, carrying a huge plastic bag. "Mind if I come in?"

I shove the letter I'm reading for the sixth time under my pillow. "You already *are* in."

"Well, look at that," Dad says, sitting on my bed. "Guess I am."

"Yeah."

"Yeah."

It's quiet for several seconds, then Dad lets out a big breath. "So, how you doing?"

Scared to death about starting school. " 'Kay. You?"

" 'Kay." He hoists the bag onto the bed. "School clothes."

Mom used to take me shopping for school clothes at Target, then to Nature's Way Café for lunch. She always ordered the sprouts and avocado sandwich on pita, and I always ordered a grilled cheese and tomato sandwich with a fruit smoothie. It was a big deal, because Mom didn't go out of the house too often.

"David?"

I shake my head. "Yeah?"

Dad pulls out three pairs of jeans—two blue, one black—that don't look too bad, two short-sleeved collared shirts and three long-sleeved collared shirts. "Remember?" Dad asks. "Dress code."

"Yup. Collared shirts. I remember." The principal's letter explaining the dress code is stuck to our fridge with the guitar magnet Mom gave Dad the day he found out that his advice column—"Alan's Answers"—was going to be nationally syndicated. "Don't forget about this part of you," Mom said, and pressed a button on the magnet, causing a guitar riff to play for about five seconds.

Dad kissed Mom on the forehead. "How could I forget, Anita?"

He forgot. His übercool Fender Strat lies in a dusty guitar case under his bed. And no one's pushed the button on that magnet since.

"And now," Dad says, ruffling my hair, "the pièce de résistance." He pulls out a gray T-shirt. "Ta-dah! Just don't wear it to school, okay?"

"No worries." On the front of the T-shirt is a TV set with these words inside the screen: "Be nice to me. I might be famous someday."

"So true," I say, puffing out my scrawny chest, which reminds me I haven't even tried to bulk up, like Jack suggested. And school starts in two days!

"Try it on," Dad says.

I can tell that my liking the T-shirt means a lot to him, so

I slip it over my head, look down at myself and say, "My new favorite shirt."

Instead of acting happy, though, Dad gets this far-off look in his eyes, like he does when someone mentions Mom.

I can't stand seeing that look, so I nudge his shoulder. "Thanks for all the great stuff."

He blinks a few times and pretend-punches me in the shoulder. "I'm sure your mom would've gotten better stuff, but . . ."

But she, um, moved to Maine to live with an organic-beet farmer two years ago. "It's perfect, Dad. Really."

"Well, I'm just going to . . ." Dad crumples the empty plastic bag and moves toward the door.

I nod.

"Okay, then."

"Yup."

He slips out of my room, and I grab the letter I was reading before he came in.

Dear David,

I can't believe it's time for school again. I wish I were there, helping you pick out your clothes (or are you too big for that now?) and having lunch with you at Nature's Way Café. I miss that place. I miss you!

Even though I'm reading this letter for the seventh time, my stomach still seizes.

I especially miss being around you and your sister at the start of a new school year. Please tell her I wish she'd answer my letters.

I blink a few times. "Maybe if you got a phone . . . ," I say to the letter and swipe at my eyes.

Well, it's getting very cool here. I'm working on another patchwork quilt to keep us warm during winter. Did I already tell you that? And I'm canning steamed beets and several pounds of string beans that Marcus got in trade from a neighbor's farm.

Good luck at school, David. I hope you have a wonderful experience at Harman. Tell your sister I wish her luck at Bensalem High.

I'm glad you write to me, David. It means a lot. You'll do great in middle school, but it can be rough. Just remember: don't break any rules, especially on the first day. (Like you'd ever do that!)

But mostly, remember how much I love you.

Peace and pancakes,

Mom

"Peace and pancakes," I mumble. "Whatever that means." I wonder why Mom had to move to a farm in Maine to "find herself." Couldn't she have found herself right here in Bensalem with us, instead of running off with the Farmer? His real name's Marcus, and he's too cheap to have a computer or a phone or even electricity in their house. Mom would have to go into town to call us, which she never does.

Lindsay says Mom's not finding herself; she says Mom's just selfish and has some sort of disorder.

I breathe hard, slip the letter back into its envelope and shove it into a shoe box in my closet, along with the other dozens of letters from Mom telling me about their organic beet crop and freezing weather and crazy quilts she makes. Mom says she sews our names into every quilt.

I'd trade the whole box of letters for one lousy visit.

7

Monday morning, Elliott's late as usual, so I tape fake New York on my wall and start making *TalkTime* without him.

After shooting the introduction, I find Lindsay and get footage of her face, which looks less zit-infested today.

"David, get out!" she screams, then throws her shoe at me.

Fortunately, I have good reflexes, and the shoe hits me, not my camera.

Back in my room, I decide that these words will go with Lindsay's face: *Today's acne forecast: sunny, with a light scattering of zits later in the day.*

Elliott's still not here, so I put the camera on the tripod and create the list segment of the show: "Top Six and a Half Ways to Survive a Summer Pool Party. One: Don't go! The other five and a half ways don't matter."

Forty-seven minutes late, Elliott finally walks through the

front door with a book in his hand. "Look," he says, and offers me his yearbook.

"You're late," I say, not taking the stupid yearbook from his stupid hand.

"Big deal," Elliott says. "I'm always late."

My nostrils flare. "It *is* a big deal. I started shooting without you."

"So what? Don't be such a jerk, David."

"Jerk? *I'm* not being a jerk."

Elliott pokes me in the chest. "Yes, *you* are being a jerk. And you were a jerk and a half at the mall on Friday."

"Me?" I say, touching the spot on my chest where he poked me. "You were a jerk and three-quarters. Maybe I didn't want to spend my entire summer at the mall looking for Cara Epstein."

"Yeah, that was dumb."

I reel back. "It was?"

"Yeah," he says. "Kind of a waste of a summer, huh?"

"Definitely." I'm glad to see a glimmer of the old Elliott. "But we've still got today. Right?"

"Right," Elliott says, and we bump fists. "Now, look." He hands me his yearbook again.

Sadly, I know right where to turn. I go to the page where Cara Epstein drew those lousy purple hearts. The entry is completely blacked out and smells of permanent marker. I close the yearbook and hand it back. "Wow."

"Cool, huh?" Elliott takes a deep breath. "You were right."

"What?"

"I said you were right."

"I know. Just wanted to hear you say it again."

Elliott punches me in the shoulder. "I need to stop thinking about Cara. I mean, we're going to middle school tomorrow, right?"

"Yup," I say, wishing I'd spent the weekend lifting weights and doing push-ups.

"And Harman will be loaded with girls, right?"

I know where he's heading. "Yeah."

"Sixth-grade girls. Seventh-grade. Eighth. Am I right?" Elliott gets a dreamy look in his eyes that totally creeps me out.

He's heading down the tracks at a hundred miles an hour. "Uh, I guess."

"So who needs Cara Epstein?" Elliott says. "She's not even going to Harman."

Toward an oncoming train.

Elliott puffs his chest out and declares, "I, Elliott Isaac Berger, am gonna make out with every single girl at Harman Middle School before I graduate!"

Crash!

"Great," I say in a less than enthusiastic tone. "Can we please get started now?"

"That was supposed to be a joke." Elliott shoves me.

"Ha," I say, pulling away.

Elliott shrugs and sprints up the stairs.

I follow him into my room. "I shot everything except the interview and a public service announcement."

"Cool," Elliott says, tapping on Hammy's cage, which annoys me. "Who are we interviewing today?"

"Ashton Kutcher."

"Awesome," Elliott says. "I can do Ashton."

"Then I wrote a public service announcement about preventing skin cancer."

"Sounds like fun." Elliott makes a face. "Can't we do something about girls instead? Like how to get them to fall madly in love with you?"

"Uh, and why would we want to do something dumb like that?"

"Because it's way better than your stupid idea."

I exhale through clenched teeth. "We're doing the Ashton Kutcher interview and the PSA about preventing skin cancer. I already wrote it."

Elliott steps back. "What if I don't want to do the stupid cancer PSA? What if I want to do the girl PSA?"

Prickly heat creeps up my neck. "What if I do the interview *and* the PSA without you?"

"What if you do? Moron."

"Supermoron."

He shoves me. "Megamoron." Then he turns away like I'm not worth looking at and mutters, "Schmo."

I breathe in short bursts. Then it pops out of my mouth, like a firecracker: "Cara Epstein drew two purple hearts in *my* yearbook."

There is electrically charged silence between us.

"Liar!"

I grab my yearbook, find the page with Cara's entry and shove it in Elliott's face. "She probably put two hearts in everybody's yearbook." I slam the book and throw it onto my bed. "Who's the schmo now?"

Elliott's lips pinch together, and he glares at me before exploding. "You suck!"

"You . . . ssssuper suck!" I breathe hard through my nose and try to think of something meaner to say. "And maybe if your dad was around, my dad wouldn't have had to drive us to the mall twenty-four times!"

Elliott's eyes open wide.

My stomach plunges. I know that was a low blow. I know better than anyone how awful it feels for a parent to up and leave. I have no idea why I just said that.

"Well, maybe if your mom—" Elliott's voice cracks, and not because his vocal cords are lengthening.

I bite my lip, wishing there were a rewind button on my mouth.

Elliott snatches his yearbook and storms out of my room.

Even though "sorry" bounces around my brain, I stand there, stupid and silent, and watch Elliott Isaac Berger, my—*gulp*—*former* best friend, stomp down the stairs and out of my house.

8 ▶

I attempt to shoot the Ashton Kutcher interview without Elliott, but my throat tightens. I hope he calls, so I can tell him I'm sorry, because I am.

I let Hammy out of his cage and pet behind his ears, which usually makes me feel better, but not today.

If Mom were here, she'd probably sit on the edge of my bed, push my hair out of my eyes and tell me to call Elliott and apologize.

And I'd tell Mom I can't call Elliott and apologize, because even though I know what I said was mean, it's Elliott's fault, too. He was a jerk all summer. I was only a jerk today.

Mom would probably tell me to call anyway. She'd talk to me about things like karma and how my spirit would be enhanced if I called and apologized. She'd remind me that Elliott's been my best friend for years.

I hold Hammy in one hand and the phone in the other, but I can't make myself press the numbers. I can't shoot the interview. I don't feel like making the PSA. This was supposed to be a great day, but it's just another lousy day in a string of lousy summer days.

9

Hammy seems completely uninterested in my plight. Until he pees on my hand.

"I deserve that." I put Hammy back into his cage and scrub my hand.

Then I reach into the back of my closet and pull out an old birthday gift from Mom. I sit on my bed and work the Rubik's Cube but can't get more than one side the same color. Mom said to close my eyes and envision myself solving the cube. I try it, but that doesn't work, either. Even when I cheat and look up how to solve it on the Internet, I get only two sides the same color.

When Bubbe calls me for dinner, I'm glad.

But when I see what we're having—creamed spinach, brown rice and liver with fried onions—I'm not glad anymore. I eat a few forkfuls of rice and move the other stuff around on my plate.

"You're quiet," Bubbe says, shoving a chunk of liver and a dangling onion into her mouth.

I don't say anything.

When the phone rings after dinner, I lunge for it, hoping it's Elliott. But Lindsay gets to it first.

"Hello?" she says, twirling a piece of hair around her finger. "Yes, I'm Ms. Greenberg."

"Liar," I mouth.

She shrugs.

"No," Lindsay says. "We don't want a year's worth of prime beef delivered fresh to our door." She bites her lower lip. "Oh, I'm sure. Our family is vegetarian. All twelve of us."

I smile.

"Even the dog," Lindsay says.

"Woof. Woof," I bark.

Lindsay hangs up and bursts out laughing. "Good dog, David." She pats my head.

I stand, do a fake bow, then grab the phone and retreat to my room.

By bedtime, I realize I'm not going to call Elliott and he's not going to call me, either, but I stay up till eleven with the phone beside my bed just in case he does.

10

When the phone rings in the morning, I smack the snooze button on my alarm clock. The ringing doesn't stop even though I smack it again and again.

"Answer the phone!" Lindsay screams, and pounds on her bedroom wall.

"Stop banging the wall!" Dad shouts, and pounds on his own wall.

That's when I realize my alarm clock doesn't ring; it beeps. I answer the phone. "Yeah?"

"Hey, buddy."

It's Elliott. He called me buddy. I try to think of something nice to say to show him I'm sorry and want to be friends again. But all that comes out is a sleepy "Hey."

"You ready for school?" Elliott asks. It sounds like he's laughing, but I'm still too tired to process much.

"Elliott," I say, wiping gunk out of my eyes, "I'm really sorry about yesterday. What I said was—"

"I'm so over that."

"Really?" I can't believe Elliott's forgiven me so easily. "But I am sorry."

"Yeah, whatever. By the way, Tommy Murphy spent the day at my place yesterday, and he let me in on something important."

My heart hammers. "Tommy Murphy?" A couple of years ago, he threw pinecones at us while we walked home from school. When Elliott turned to tell him to quit, Tommy nailed him in the head with a rock. Elliott's forehead bled like crazy, so his mom called a doctor friend. She told Elliott's mom to stick Elliott's skin back together with Krazy Glue. *Krazy Glue!* And it worked, except Elliott still has a scar. "*The* Tommy Murphy?"

"Yeah," Elliott says.

"The one who lives in your apartment building?"

"Duh. What other Tommy Murphy is there, David?"

"But I thought—"

I hear muffled laughter.

"What's that?"

"What's what?" Elliott coughs.

I don't hear anything else. "So what did Tommy let you in on?"

"Okay," Elliott says. "You know that whole dress code thing?"

"Yeah."

"Tommy told me all the kids are purposely breaking it today."

"Breaking it?" My voice cracks. "All the kids?"

"You know, the seventh and eighth graders and the cool sixth graders."

I remember Mom's letter. *Don't break any rules, especially on the first day.* "But—"

"I'm definitely wearing a T-shirt," Elliott says. "You should, too."

"Really?" I whisper, as though the Dress Code Police can hear me.

"David, if you *don't* wear a T-shirt today, the eighth graders are going to target you for the rest of the year."

"No!" Everything Jack said rushes back. "I don't want to be a target."

"Exactly," Elliott says. "That's why I'm looking out for you, buddy."

"Thanks, but do you really think . . . ?" I bite my bottom lip.

"Yeah," Elliott says. "Everyone's doing it."

"But I thought—"

"Relax, David. This is a no-brainer. You don't want to be labeled a dork your first day, do you?"

"No, but—"

"So you'll wear a T-shirt today?"

I swallow hard and push Jack's and Mom's words from my mind. "Yeah. I'll wear one." I slide out of bed, wondering how I'll sneak past Dad. "So, Elliott, you coming to my house or you want me to walk to yours?"

"Uh, I promised Tommy I'd walk with him."

My stomach squeezes, but since Elliott's being such a good guy about everything, I make a concession. "I can meet both of you at your place, then." Silence. "I mean, if that's okay." *Why wouldn't it be?*

"Look, David, how about we meet you in the school's courtyard?"

"But—"

"Just wear your T-shirt and meet us in the courtyard."

Before I click off the phone, I know exactly which T-shirt I'll wear.

11

In Dad's office, the computer casts a ghostly blue glow on his face.

"Poor woman," Dad says. "Wants to keep homeschooling her daughter because she's afraid if she goes to school, she'll be lonely at home without her. Can you imagine?"

"Um, not really," I say.

Dad pushes away from his computer. "I'm suggesting she find activities during the day with people of her own age. Maybe get a job. Or volunteer somewhere."

"Um, great advice," I say, wishing I hadn't interrupted Dad's work on his advice column.

"Oh my gosh." Dad looks at his watch. "I didn't realize . . ."

"Yup." I bob from foot to foot.

"First day of middle school!" Dad comes around his desk and examines me from head to toe.

I hold my breath. *Please don't notice.*

"Looking good," Dad says, even though it's obvious my hair is sticking out in weird ways.

I let my breath out. "Thanks."

"Want a ride to Elliott's?" Dad nods toward his computer. "My column can wait. Or is he coming here?"

I take a step back. "We're meeting at school."

"Too big to meet at each other's houses," Dad says, as though he understands some great truth.

He doesn't.

"For lunch." Dad hands me a five. "Now, go forth and conquer."

I back up and reach for the doorknob. "Going forth." I swallow hard. "And conquering."

Dad returns to his desk. "All right, Perplexed in Pennsylvania," he says, positioning his fingers on the keyboard. "Alan's answer is on its way, but you probably won't like it."

"Bye, Dad."

He glances up. "Hey, that shirt looks good on you. Your old man has decent taste, huh?"

I gulp down guilt. "Yup." Easing out of Dad's office, I close the door and run upstairs. After stripping off my collared shirt, I throw it onto the bed and head back downstairs, wearing the T-shirt Dad gave me.

I feel sorry for the dorky sixth graders who won't know about the T-shirt thing. I'm lucky Elliott gave me the heads-up. Still, as I walk toward Harman, I feel sort of naked.

Two guys run past me and shove each other. They're wearing collared shirts. I squint. They don't look like dorky sixth graders.

The closer I get to Harman, the more kids I see and the

heavier my feet feel. By the time I reach the crossing guard at the intersection before school, my feet are fifteen-pound bowling balls.

Breathe, David. Breathe!

When the crossing guard blows her whistle and motions me to walk, I force my bowling-ball feet to carry me across the intersection, even though what I want to do is run home.

Harman's courtyard is flooded with kids, some hugging each other, some shoving and some standing alone. Everyone is wearing a collared shirt.

Correction: one really heavy guy, who is definitely not a sixth grader, wears a T-shirt that reads "I may be fat, but you're ugly and I can diet." *Definitely not dress code.*

As I search for Elliott, a girl points at me—or, more specifically, at my T-shirt—and whispers to a girl beside her. Then they both giggle.

Elliott Berger, I'm going to KILL you for making me wear this stupid T-shirt!

A loud buzzer sounds, and everyone funnels toward two open doors. I'm being pushed along, my heart pounding because I don't want to be one of only two kids to enter Harman Middle School the first day wearing a T-shirt.

That's when I see Elliott's face next to Tommy's. I let out a breath, because I know that Elliott will be wearing his "It's not my fault" T-shirt, and we can stick together today. The girl in front of Elliott moves out of the way, so I have a good view of him and Tommy.

They're both wearing collared shirts.

12

The cafeteria smells like mold. I try not to breathe, but that makes me dizzy.

Kids form lines in front of tables along one wall. There are signs behind the tables with letters: A–G, H–P and Q–Z.

A bald guy walks around with a megaphone and bellows, "Line up in front of the letter that starts your last name. When you receive your schedule, head directly to your first-period class. You'll find maps along the walls."

I'm supposed to stand in the "A–G" line.

So is Elliott.

Instead, I stand near a bulletin board with a poster that reads

Harman students are . . .
Always prepared, positive and proud
Responsible and respectful

Making excellent choices
Academically astonishing
Neat, careful and considerate citizens.

I pretend to study the poster but am secretly spying on Elliott. When there are seven kids behind him, I decide it's safe to get in line.

I shoot vaporizing rays at the back of Elliott's head. *I hope you aren't in any of my classes. I hope you make out with some eighth-grade girl and get suspended. Or beaten up. Or both!*

"Nice shirt," Elliott says as he walks past, holding his schedule.

I watch Elliott catch up with Tommy. They compare schedules and walk out of the cafeteria. Together.

When it's my turn at the table, the lady says, "Name?"

"David."

"Last?"

I look behind me. There is no one else.

"Last?" she says more loudly.

"Um, yes, I am."

She closes her eyelids. When she opens them again, she tilts her head and says, "Last *name?*"

I want to say *Moron* because that's what I feel like.

"Greenberg. My last name is Greenberg. And my middle name is Todd, after—"

"Here you go," she says, handing me the schedule. "You have Ms. Lovely first period."

"Ms. Lovely?"

"Yes." The lady looks tired. Of me.

I turn to go just as the man with the megaphone says something near my ear. "Please go immediately to your first-period class."

I check the room number on my schedule and run out of the cafeteria.

A teacher stops me. "Whoa. No running."

"Sorry," I say. "I'm late."

"That's okay. It's the first day."

I shove my schedule at him. "Can you tell me how to get to"—I feel funny saying the name—"Ms. Lovely's math class?"

"End of that hall." He points.

"Thanks." I walk quickly.

Behind me, I'm sure I hear him mutter, "Good luck."

13

A harsh buzz sounds as I enter the classroom.

The first thing I see is Tommy Murphy in the back row. I picture Tommy hoisting some scrawny kid over a railing. And the kid falling, his arms and legs flailing. I can almost hear the thump as his honeydew head hits the floor and cracks open.

I scan the room. All the kids look bigger than me, except one girl in the front row, who has red curly hair. I slide into the empty seat beside her.

I knew they were moving me up to seventh-grade math this year because of my standardized test scores, but Tommy Murphy is in *eighth* grade. *Am I in the wrong room?*

The red-haired girl smiles at me.

I nod, thinking it's the cool thing to do.

She nods back and whispers, "I like your T-shirt."

I sit up taller. *Thank you, Elliott Berger.*

Ms. Lovely, a petite woman in a dress, turns from the board.

My lower jaw dangles. That can't be Ms. *Lovely*.

This woman makes Bubbe look young. Her skin is so tanned and wrinkled that her face looks like the hindquarters of an elephant.

"Welcome to math class," the woman says in a raspy voice. She sounds like she spent her life working at the Smokin' and Chokin' Cigarette Factory. "I'm your teacher, Ms. Lovely."

The red-haired girl and I exchange panicked glances.

Ms. Lovely parks herself in front of my desk. "You're in Math II. This class is for seventh-grade students." She glares at Tommy Murphy. "For the most part."

I look back and see Tommy sink low in his seat. He must have failed math last year.

Ms. Lovely's raspy voice invades my thoughts. "We do have two sixth-grade students in our class. They tested exceptionally well."

I sink low in my seat, too, and notice that the red-haired girl does the same.

Ms. Lovely is beaming, though, which makes her wrinkles even deeper. "We could all learn from their dedication."

I glance at the red-haired girl. Her eyelids are closed.

A rude noise erupts from the back. I'm sure it came from Tommy.

Ms. Lovely raises one eyebrow, and the room falls silent.

"You," Ms. Lovely says in her gravelly voice, pointing at my chest.

I put a hand over my heart and look around.

"Yes, you," she rasps. "Stand."

When I stand, my legs feel like wet matzo. *Maybe she's going to announce my math test score from last year—99 percent. That will be humiliating.*

"This," she croaks, pointing at my chest, "is a flagrant demonstration of *not* following school dress code. Come up here."

Elliott Berger, I hate you!

I step from behind my desk, feeling kids watch me. My cheeks grow so warm I'm sure I'll spontaneously combust and turn into a pile of ash right in front of the class. At least, I hope so.

Ms. Lovely nods toward my T-shirt. "You're famous, all right, Mr. . . . ," she croaks in a very unlovely way.

It takes a moment for me to realize she's waiting for my last name.

"Greenberg." My voice cracks. Curse my lengthening vocal cords!

"Look around, Mr. Greenberg. Do you see others wearing T-shirts in this classroom?"

I look around but already know what I'll see. "No."

"Of course not. In this room and in this school, Mr. Greenberg, we follow the rules."

I can see Mom's letter in my mind. *Don't break any rules, especially on the first day.*

Ms. Lovely pokes me with her clawlike finger.

I cringe and slide back into my seat.

Elliott Berger, I'm going to kill you!

14

The noise in the cafeteria is rock-band loud. It smells like sloppy joes and mold.

I'm hungry, and the line to buy food is long. I stand at the end of it, then touch the five-dollar bill from Dad in my pocket. The kid in front of me turns and says, "David!"

It's Gavin from Longwood El. He and I were in Academic Games together last year.

"Yo, Gavin," I say, high-fiving him. We both look around to make sure no one saw, in case that's something you shouldn't do in middle school.

"What's up?" Gavin asks.

I think of the humiliating T-shirt incident in Ms. Lovely's class, cross my arms over my chest and say, "Not much. What's up with you?"

He shrugs. "Nothing much."

We stare at each other and nod; then Gavin turns back

around and I feel alone again. It takes forever for me to move up to the front of the line.

"Ewww. Gloppy joe," a kid behind me says.

I stare at the silver pans full of sloppy—um, gloppy—joe and something that I think is spinach. There's also a tray of sliced carrots. My stomach makes an embarrassing noise.

"Before tomorrow," the lunch lady says, brandishing her long metal spoon.

"Carrots and sloppy joe, please." *This lady won't be slipping me free ice cream on Fridays.*

I grip my red plastic tray and scan the cafeteria. Other than Gavin, I don't recognize anyone. That's why Elliott and I were supposed to stick together—because there weren't going to be a lot of us coming from Longwood El. Most of the kids at Harman come from Trailside El because of the dumb boundary rules. Gavin is already talking and laughing with a bunch of guys I don't know, so I sit at a table near the door and dig my plastic spork into the gloppy joe.

My mouth is full when I see Elliott walking toward me. Even though I hate what he did to me this morning, I feel a tiny spark of hope that he'll sit with me. We could work this whole thing out and be friends again by next period.

I notice Tommy beside Elliott, and the spark dims. *What is he doing with that Neanderthal?*

"Yo, David," Elliott says, as though we're still best buds.

"Yo, Dave," Tommy says, like a brain-damaged parrot.

Elliott rests his tray on my table. He chose the same food I did; we both hate spinach. "So, how's the T-shirt thing working out for you?" Elliott asks. Tommy laughs so hard he snorts.

The memory of Ms. Lovely embarrassing me in front of the class, in front of the red-haired girl, crashes back.

It's all your fault.

I turn and laser-focus on Elliott, who has picked up his tray and has this innocent *who me?* look on his face.

It's all your fault!

Elliott's eyes open wide.

I realize that his eyes look panicked because I'm off my seat and in his face. Kids from other tables swivel around to watch.

Tommy steps forward.

Elliott tugs on his shirt collar—*his shirt collar!*—and says, "What?"

"You're a jerk," I say, and shove Elliott's tray so hard it smashes onto the front of his shirt and knocks him backward.

"What the—"

Elliott's sitting on the floor, looking up and blinking while globs of food cling to the front of his shirt. A sliced carrot slips down his neck. Elliott's mouth moves, but no sound comes out.

I back up, every muscle tense. "I'm sorry. I—"

Elliott scrambles off the floor. He charges toward me, slips on something and slams into me.

I fall backward and land hard on my butt.

"Jerk!" I scream, rocketing up toward Elliott.

He hits me hard on the side of the head.

I swing, landing a fist square on his cheek. "I hate you!" I yell, but it's drowned out by chanting.

"Fight. Fight. *Fight.*"

Could they be talking about me? David "Please Don't Hit Me" Greenberg?

Elliott lands one hard on my chin.

I blink a few times and am pulling my fist back just as someone grabs my arms and yanks.

I'm still trying to swing when I look over my shoulder and see that the person holding me is the police officer. *The police officer is holding me!*

"I'm sorry . . . i-it's just . . . ," I stammer.

Her grip tightens.

Elliott struggles against the man holding him, and I can't believe how much he looks like he wants to kill me.

The cafeteria falls whisper-quiet as the bald guy who had the megaphone this morning charges over. He nods at the police officer. "I'll take it from here."

When the officer loosens her grip, the bald guy grabs my arm. It hurts.

Elliott breathes through flaring nostrils, like a bull ready to charge.

I glance around at kids staring at me and bite my lower lip.

"Take him to the nurse," the bald guy says to the man holding Elliott. "Then make sure he gets to my office. I'll have to call his parents."

Parent, I want to say. *Elliott has one parent.*

As he's being led away, Elliott glowers at me, food splattered on his collared shirt and a fat red mark on his cheek. I look down, knowing I ruined Elliott's first day of school, too.

Tommy stands nearby, grinning.

"Let's go," the bald man says, tightening his grip on my already sore arm.

15

It turns out Mr. Carp (aka Bald Guy) is the assistant principal for sixth grade.

I know this because there is a sign on his desk that reads MR. CARP, SIXTH-GRADE ASSISTANT PRINCIPAL.

"What do you have to say for yourself, Mr. . . ." He runs his hand over the freckled skin on his scalp.

"Greenberg."

"What do you have to say, Mr. Greenberg?"

"Uh, I'm really sorry."

Mr. Carp nods. "I'll bet you are, son." And he picks up the phone.

Actually, I'm not that sorry. Because I, David Todd Greenberg, biggest fraidy cat ever, was in my first fight. And I think I might have won!

I'll never tell Mr. Carp this, but I feel a little proud of myself.

Until Dad shows up.

16

Dad skids into Mr. Carp's office, breathing hard.

I sink low in my chair, feeling smaller than ever.

"Mr. Greenberg?" Mr. Carp says to him.

Dad shakes Mr. Carp's hand but looks at me. "What's this about a fight, David?"

I can tell by the look in Dad's eyes that he's hoping it's a mistake, that some other David Greenberg was dumb enough to get into a fight the first day of school.

"It's j-just—" I stammer.

"And why are you wearing *that?*" Dad points to my T-shirt. "I thought I made it clear—"

"Mr. Greenberg?" Mr. Carp points to the chair next to mine.

Dad sits and runs his hand through his hair.

"I've looked into David's file," Mr. Carp says. "It's obvious he's a good kid. A really good kid."

Dad's face softens a little.

"Sometimes, starting middle school can be rough."

"You can say that again," I mutter.

They both glare at me, and my cheeks get warm.

Mr. Carp continues. "But David made a mistake."

"A big mistake!" Dad says, looking directly into my eyes.

I sink lower in my chair.

Mr. Carp puts both palms on his desk. "Here's what we're going to do. Mr. Greenberg, you're going to take David home. We'll call it a one-day suspension."

The word "suspension" kicks my heart into overdrive.

"Okay," Dad says, the vein on the side of his head pulsing.

"And he's going to come to school tomorrow wearing a collared shirt."

"Of course," Dad says, giving me a look.

"And he's going to stay out of trouble all year." Mr. Carp looks at me. "Isn't that right, David?"

"That's right," I say.

Mr. Carp offers me his hand, and I shake it even though my palm is sweaty. Then he shakes Dad's hand and picks up the phone. "Send the other boy in now."

As Dad and I walk out of Mr. Carp's office, Elliott walks in.

His shirt is soaked and covered with food stains.

I know that's probably the only new shirt Elliott got this year. His mom rarely has money for extras like school clothes. And whatever he gets has to last all year, even if he outgrows it. Even if his former best friend ruins it with a tray full of gloppy joe and sliced carrots. I have the word "sorry" on my lips, but Elliott glares at me. If he had death-ray vision, I'd be vaporized. Then, secretly, he nods toward his hand, which is curled into a fist.

He lifts his middle finger. At me!

I don't care that I ruined his stupid shirt anymore.

In Dad's car in the parking lot, my shoulders relax a little, until I look over at him. There's a deep crease above his eyebrows, and he's gripping the steering wheel even though he hasn't started the car yet.

Dad turns to me, glances at my T-shirt, then looks up at my eyes and says six soft words that pierce my heart.

"David, I'm so disappointed in you."

17

When we walk into the house, I say, "Dad, Elliott tricked me into wearing a T-shirt today."

Dad swivels and levels me with a stare. "Tricked you? *Tricked you?* First of all, David, you're smarter than that. Second, I don't care if Elliott told you to dance naked on Mr. Carp's bald head. You had no right to do that. Elliott doesn't have it so easy, you know."

Neither do I!

"What the heck were you thinking?" Dad doesn't wait for an answer. He shakes his head and stalks toward his office.

"Thanks for being such a good listener," I mumble, and trudge upstairs.

Even though I know that Lindsay's at school, I get a sinking feeling when I open her door and see that her bed's made and her room's empty. Downstairs, Bubbe's apartment is quiet, and I remember it's her day to volunteer at the library.

The person I really feel like talking to is probably still in

Mr. Carp's office. His mom isn't going to be able to get there as fast as Dad did. Ms. Berger is going to be pissed about having to leave work to get him. I've heard her say to Elliott about a million times, "If I don't work, I don't get paid."

"It's not my fault," I whisper.

In the living room, I plop onto the couch, take a deep breath and look at Mom's tuba. It looks lonely. My plastic tub of K'nex pieces sits on the floor next to it. I never put it away after that first day of summer, when Elliott and I went to the dumb mall instead of building something cool.

I pick up the red tub, and even though I think I'm carrying it upstairs to put back in my closet, I detour to the garage. I don't turn on the light, so it's dark, and it's smelly as I lift the garbage can lid. K'nex pieces cascade against each other into the can. Then I drop the empty tub into the recycling bin and head to my room.

When I open my bedroom door, the first thing I see is the collared shirt from this morning. I hurl it to the floor, stretch out on my bed, glance at Hammy and remember the day Mom gave him to me. "Someone to love," she said, handing me a trembling ball of fur. "I popped into Pet Palace for a minute and he looked so . . . so . . . lonely."

A few days after that, Mom left.

I wonder if Mom got me Hammy because she knew I'd be lonely soon.

My throat tightens. I bite my lip, staving off tears, and remind myself that middle schoolers don't cry over K'nex pieces and ex–best friends. And they definitely don't cry about missing their moms.

I drag myself off the bed and take Hammy out of his cage. His whiskers twitch, and he seems happy to see me. *At least someone is.*

There's a knock on the door. I hold my breath and say nothing, because even if Dad is ready to talk to me, I don't feel like talking to him anymore.

My door creaks open, and Bubbe pokes her head in. "May I come in, *bubelah?*"

I shrug. When she calls me *bubelah*, it makes me feel safe and babyish at the same time.

Bubbe sits on the edge of my bed, looks into my eyes and pushes hair off my forehead, like Mom used to. "Bubelah," she says, squeezing my knee, "your father told me what happened."

I open my mouth to explain, but Bubbe isn't finished.

"I'm sorry your first day went like that, Davey."

Davey. Does she have to call me Davey? The air leaks out of me, and my chest heaves.

Bubbe takes Hammy from my hands and puts him into his cage. She comes back to the bed and holds me in her arms just as Niagara Falls gushes out of my eyes.

"It was horrible," I say into her shirt. "Ms. Lovely's horrible. Elliott's . . ." I blubber against Bubbe's chest and my nose runs.

She rocks me and says, "Sha! Sha, bubelah. It'll be okay. You'll see."

Even though I know that Bubbe is wrong and it won't be okay, it's nice to hear those words.

I just wish they were coming from Mom.

18

The next morning, I wake exactly twenty-three minutes before my alarm is set to buzz, because our phone won't stop ringing.

"Get the phone!" Lindsay yells.

"Stop yelling," Dad yells.

"Stop yelling at me to stop yelling!"

I grab the phone and push the talk button. "Hello?"

"Hey, David."

The voice makes my heart pound.

"David?" Tommy Murphy asks. "That's you, right?"

I hold my breath, remembering Jack's warning about staying away from Tommy. *That kid's crazy mean.*

A familiar voice in the background says, "It's him."

"Okay, then," Tommy says. "Wanted you to know everyone at Harman's wearing a bathing suit today. It's Bathing Suit Day!"

I hold my breath and press the phone against my ear.

"So, make sure you wear the one with penguins all over it."

Before I can find the off button in the dark, I hear Elliott and Tommy cracking up.

I hurl the phone across my room and pull my knees to my chest.

Hammy startles.

"Sorry, Ham," I say, my voice catching.

Elliott was here when Mom gave me that bathing suit. He saw how excited she was to find one covered with her favorite animal—penguins. Penguins skiing, penguins sledding and penguins building snowmen . . . on swim trunks. I thought they were funny until I wore them to Aunt Sherry's pool party. Elliott came with us that year. He stood next to me when Jack said, "Cute suit, David. Does it come with a swim diaper?"

When we got home, I shoved the bathing suit to the very back of my underwear drawer and made Elliott promise—promise!—he wouldn't tell another human being about those stupid trunks. Granted, Tommy Murphy is not exactly a human being, but still . . .

After that, Mom started buying penguin everything. She gave me penguin earmuffs. Lindsay got penguin earrings, penguin school folders and seven pairs of penguin pajamas. Dad got penguin boxer shorts in six different colors, and tiny penguin statues began appearing all over the place. Mom bought a dozen copies of Mr. Popper's Penguins and scattered them throughout the house.

Once, during dinner, Mom left the table and called the Philadelphia Zoo. When I heard her ask about buying a real penguin, I got excited. I thought it would be fun to have a penguin, except we'd probably have to keep the air conditioner blasting, even in winter. Dad got up so fast his chair fell over. He grabbed the phone from Mom's hand, hung up and started screaming about responsibility and reality. Lindsay kept eating.

I yank the blanket over my head and moan. "Elliott, you lousy, stinkin', rotten . . . !"

What if Tommy Murphy tells everyone at school about my penguin bathing suit? What if the red-haired girl finds out? What if Tommy throws me over a railing?

I pull the blanket off my head and watch light stream through the window.

"I should tell everyone that Elliott slept with Boo-Boo Bear until he was ten and a half," I say to Hammy. "But *I* am too nice to do something like that!"

19

Before I leave for school, Dad checks underneath my collared shirt.

"Don't worry," I say, pulling away. "I'm not going to do that again."

"I know." Dad ruffles my hair. "You're a good kid, David. You just had a bad day."

On the way to school, something hits me between the shoulder blades.

I whirl around, expecting to see Tommy Murphy holding a rock in one hand and my penguin bathing suit in the other, which is ridiculous, because the suit is still stashed in my underwear drawer. I know this because after the phone call, I checked. Didn't want to find it flying on the flagpole at school this morning.

"Sorry," a kid says, and runs past. "I was aiming for him." He scoops up a pinecone and chucks it at some guy.

"Not even close!" the guy screams, and runs off.

Watching them makes me miss walking to school with El-liott. He used to tell the lamest jokes, like "What's the difference between middle school and a loony bin? Nothing." Even when Tommy Murphy chucked pinecones at us, at least Elliott and I were together—a team—fighting the forces of evil. Now Elliott *is* a force of evil, and all I'm left with is a big empty space in my stomach that feels like it will never be filled.

In the courtyard, I'm relieved about two things.

Thing One: I'm dressed like everyone else, in a collared shirt.

Thing Two: I don't see Elliott or Tommy anywhere.

I bump into a boy and say, "Excuse me."

"No sweat," he says, and hoists his backpack onto his shoulder.

I look around. Everyone seems to have gotten the backpack memo. What other vital information have I missed? Maybe back-pack info was given out Tuesday afternoon, after Mr. Carp sent me home. *What if there was homework assigned in some of my classes, and I'll be marked as unprepared?*

"Hey!"

I whirl around and stumble.

The red-haired girl covers her mouth and giggles. "New feet?"

My cheeks burn. "No, um . . ." *Ask her name.*

"We're in math together. Remember?" she says. "The only sixth graders."

"Yeah."

She bobs from foot to foot. "So, how's it going?"

" 'Kay," I say. " *'Kay"? Way to impress her with your one-syllable response, David!*

"So . . . ," she says, biting her bottom lip.

Say something, David! Say something or she'll walk away, and you'll be standing by yourself again. "No backpack, huh?" I want to smash myself in the forehead. *"No backpack, huh?" Way to point out the girl's deficiencies.*

"Guess we missed the memo," she says.

"Guess so." I rock back on my heels. *Ask her name, you idiot!* "By the way, what's—"

The buzzer sounds so sharply it cuts through my words.

She clutches her notebook to her chest with her left arm, bends forward and covers her ear with her right hand. "That's sooooo loud."

I cover one ear, too, to show solidarity. "Yeah," I say in yet another brilliant demonstration of my use of one-syllable words.

The red-haired girl doesn't seem to notice my extreme dorkiness, because she says, "Want to walk to math together?"

Do I want to walk to math together? "Oh, yeah!" I say, a little too enthusiastically.

As we funnel toward the doors with the crowd, I smell peppermint on her skin and get goose bumps all over my arms.

She smiles.

"You're not from Longwood El, um, Elementary, are you?" I ask as we're jostled through the doors and into the building. I know she's not from Longwood El, because I would have noticed her.

"Nope." She shakes her head, which makes her curls swing near my face.

They look so soft and . . . *Snap out of it, David!* "Trailside El?"

She shakes her head again.

We're in the hall now, walking toward Ms. Lovely's class.

"Private school?"

"Nope."

I bite my lip and think. "You just moved here?"

"Nope." She giggles and covers her mouth. "Guess again."

Before we enter Ms. Lovely's room, I step closer to the girl and hope Elliott's in the area and sees me. If he notices me standing this close to a girl who's actually talking to me, he'll be so impressed.

"Hmm," I say so she'll know I'm thinking about my next guess.

In the crush to get into Ms. Lovely's room, someone steps on the back of my sneaker. I turn around to say sorry, even though it's not my fault, but only a strangled sound comes out.

Tommy Murphy towers over me like Mount Kilimanjaro towers over an anthill.

My stomach cramps violently, and it takes all my willpower not to double over, vomit and faint. But I can't vomit or faint, because the red-haired girl is standing in front of me, and she probably wouldn't appreciate either of those things happening in her general vicinity.

Tommy whispers two words—"Penguin Boy"—near my ear, then slides into his seat at the back of the room.

I shiver and take my seat in the front row, next to the red-haired girl.

"Guess again," she says.

What were we talking about? I glance behind me. Tommy glares at me.

I face front and grip the sides of my desk.

"Hello?" the girl says. "Do you give up?"

"What?"

She presses her lips together, like she's thinking hard about something, then whispers, "Okay, I'll tell you. I was home-schooled."

"Homeschooled?" I say, more loudly than I meant to.

Panic in her eyes, she puts her finger to her lips and sinks low.

"Sorry," I whisper.

I glance back, and Tommy is quietly facing front. The chatter in the room has stopped. There's only the sound of one pencil tapping. It's my pencil.

Standing in front of my desk is Ms. Lovely. I meet her eyes. If it's possible, she looks even more tanned, wrinkled and menacing than yesterday.

And she's glaring. At me.

I'm wearing a collared shirt. I offer a weak smile. *She must teach lots of classes. Maybe she won't remember me.*

"Mr. Greenberg," she says in her gravelly voice, "no talking in my classroom unless you're answering a question."

I nod.

"And one more thing."

Oh, please strike me dead.

"Nice shirt."

Did she just wink at me?

Ms. Lovely turns on a TV suspended from the ceiling in the corner of the room.

I remember to breathe.

On the screen, a series of images appear—the front of the school, kids eating in the cafeteria, a student crossing a finish line, rows of bookshelves, a trophy case—while upbeat music plays in the background. The final image is the school's sign: HARMAN MIDDLE SCHOOL—A SAFE PLACE TO ACHIEVE ACADEMIC EXCELLENCE.

As I watch, I feel Tommy glaring holes through the back of my head.

On TV, a girl says, "Good morning, I'm Ellen Winser. Today is Wednesday, September eighth. Please stand tall for the pledge." A flag appears on the screen, and chairs scrape as everyone rises to recite the pledge.

Before Ellen Winser finishes telling us what's for lunch today, Ms. Lovely snaps off the TV and grabs a stack of papers from her desk. "This is a quick quiz," she croaks. "You should already know this material. It's a way for me to learn what you remember from last year. Pencils out."

There's a collective groan along with the sound of backpack zippers.

When Ms. Lovely distributes the quizzes, I lean toward the red-haired girl and whisper, "What's your name?" I'm grateful my voice doesn't crack.

She leans over and whispers her pepperminty name in my ear.

My whole body erupts in goose bumps.

So Fee. What an unusual name. *So Fee.* What a great name.

So Fee. So Fee. So Fee. I'm floating on a cloud of So Fee when Ms. Lovely croaks, "You may begin."

My cloud disperses.

I try to pay attention to the quiz, but I keep thinking about writing "So Fee" in the blank spaces between math problems. I shake my head and force myself to focus.

When I put my pencil down, I glance around the room and see that So Fee is the only other one finished. I smile.

When everyone's finally done, Ms. Lovely croaks, "Please trade quiz papers with your neighbor."

Too embarrassed to look at So Fee, I turn toward my left, but before I can ask the guy next to me to trade, So Fee taps my arm.

"Want to trade?" she asks.

Yeah! I shrug and hand her my paper.

When she gives me hers, our fingers touch, and I shiver. I read her name on the top line—Sophie Meyers. *Sophie Meyers and David Greenberg. Sophie Meyers Greenberg. Sophie Greenberg.*

"Penguin Boy."

I shrink down in my seat.

"Mr. Murphy," Ms. Lovely croaks. "Do you have some great wisdom to share with the class?"

I don't dare turn around, but I imagine Tommy, red-faced, shaking his head.

"Well, then," Ms. Lovely says, "perhaps you'll refrain from interrupting as I read the answers."

Tommy is silent while Ms. Lovely reads.

I put tiny check marks next to each correct answer and feel happy when I circle her score: *100.*

Sophie hands my paper back. "Congratulations, David."

Her soft words make my stomach flop around.

"Um, same to you, Sophie Meyers." But I'm thinking, *So Fee My Errs*, so I'll pronounce everything right.

Sophie put a bunch of stars around my hundred. *Does that mean she thinks I'm smart? Does she . . . could she . . . like me? Or maybe she's just a big fan of astronomy and likes stars.*

I remember Elliott obsessing over Cara Epstein's purple hearts, and for the first time, I get it.

I wish I could tell Elliott about Sophie's stars.

20

I trudge to the cafeteria, wishing that Sophie Meyers shared my lunch period or I had at least one person to sit with.

The lunch lady dumps a corn dog, baked beans and wilted lettuce on my tray.

In the lunchroom, I spot Gavin. Like yesterday, he's at a table with a bunch of guys I don't know, but I realize I need to make some friends or I'll be sitting by myself at lunch every day. Gripping the sides of my plastic tray, I stand behind Gavin and say, "Hey, Gavin, mind if I sit here?"

Everyone's talking so loudly that no one looks up.

I squeeze my tray more tightly and shout, "Hey, sit, mind if I Gavin here?"

Everyone stops talking.

A couple of guys look at me with their heads tilted. Others laugh.

I close my eyes, then slowly say, "Hey, guys, mind if I sit here?" My face flushes. At least my voice didn't crack.

I brace myself for Gavin to laugh and say, "No way, Penguin Boy; you can't even talk right."

What he does is look around the table and say, "Oh, sorry, David. There's no room left."

Why didn't I realize there was a butt on every single seat at the table before I made a fool of myself?

"That's cool." I nod. "Next time."

"Definitely," Gavin says, then goes back to talking with the guys. I hurry along the row and put my tray down at a table with only a few kids. They don't even look up.

But while I'm shoving the rubbery corn dog into my mouth, a couple of kids look past me. I turn to see Elliott and Tommy standing there, holding trays.

Is that a bruise on Elliott's cheek? It's purple; it must be a bruise.

I turn back and look at my food. *Go away.*

"Hey," Tommy says.

I squeeze my eyelids closed.

"Hey," he says more loudly, and shoves his tray into my back.

I swallow hard and turn to face them.

Tommy slings an arm over Elliott's shoulders. "Elliott showed me some of your lame videos yesterday."

Elliott nods.

I imagine the two of them looking at my videos and making fun of me.

Tommy shoves his tray into my back again. "What do you think you are, a celebrity or something?"

"Uh, no," I hear myself say, heat creeping up my neck and into the tips of my ears.

"You're lame," Tommy says. "That's what you are. Lame."

Elliott laughs. "So, David, how's your *mom* doing?"

My stomach plunges like I dropped down a roller coaster. I can't believe that Elliott brought up my mom. He knows how sad I was after she left. But then . . . I know how much talking about his dad hurts him. And I still made that stupid crack the other day.

Elliott takes a step closer. "I hear she's working so hard she's beat. Get it? Beet farm? She's beat?"

I no longer miss Elliott or his dumb jokes.

"Yeah, beat," Tommy says. "You're lame and she's beat."

"High five," Elliott says, and they high-five each other. *For making fun of my mom!*

It takes all my willpower to keep my butt on the seat and not give Elliott a fat purple bruise on his other cheek, but I have a feeling that if I tried it, Tommy would pulverize me.

How can Elliott hang out with Tommy Murphy, the guy responsible for the scar on his forehead? And how could he have told him about my penguin bathing suit and showed him our videos?

Their laughter fades as they walk away, and I finally swallow the food that's been squirreled in my cheek. The other kids at my table look down at their food. One girl hides behind a book.

I wish I could shrink to the size of a baked bean and hide on my tray until lunch is over.

Someone nudges me.

I tense and turn.

"Hey, David," Scotty Griswald says from the next table. Since our last names both start with "G," we always had to sit near each other at Longwood El. But Scotty's a superjock and I'm . . . not.

"Yeah?" I say.

Scotty leans close. "I thought Elliott Berger was your best friend. You guys always hung out together."

Elliott sits a few tables away with Tommy and a bunch of other guys, laughing. Probably at me.

I shrug at Scotty, like it's no big deal, but there's a lump the size of a matzo ball lodged in my throat.

"*Was* my best friend," I say, my voice catching on the last word.

21

After lunch, I feel like the new kid in every class. I have to ask my teachers where I sit, which is totally embarrassing, because everyone already figured that out yesterday. And in world cultures, we had homework, so I am unprepared, but Ms. Daniels says she'll let it slide if I turn in the assignment—finding out where my grandparents came from—to her tomorrow.

In science, Mr. Milot tells me to sit at a lab table near the front of the room. A lab table with four stools, three of which are already occupied by two guys I don't know and one girl I do.

"Hi, David," Sophie says, moving her notebook out of my way.

"Fancy meeting you here." Yes, I actually say this, but it's okay, because it makes Sophie giggle.

Mr. Milot drops four papers onto each table. "Quick quiz," he says, "to make sure you remember the safety rules I went over yesterday."

Safety rules? When Mr. Milot is in the back of the room, I lean toward Sophie—she still smells pepperminty—and I whisper, "What's with teachers giving so many quizzes in middle school?"

She giggles again.

When I read the questions, my stomach aches. I know four of the ten answers. *Four!* I look around and see other kids bent over their papers, scribbling. I can't get a failing quiz grade.

Sophie's paper is exposed, her answers showing. I'm about to look back at my own paper when Sophie pushes hers a little closer to me. And nods.

While Mr. Milot arranges supplies in a cabinet at the back of the room, I copy Sophie's answers. Even though I'll probably get a good grade now, I feel awful. In only two days of middle school, I've managed to get into a fight, get suspended, cheat on a quiz and, if you must know, have a few impure thoughts about Sophie.

I've got to shape up!

Mr. Milot says, "I want you to pick one person to team up with for our first project of the marking period."

I look around and see everyone else looking around, too.

"It's okay if you don't know the person," Mr. Milot says. "In fact, it's probably better."

I feel a soft touch on my arm.

When I turn, I'm looking into the green—*green!*—eyes of Sophie Meyers.

"Want to pair up, David?"

I know she's talking about the project, but it feels like something more.

"Yes," I say, mortified when my voice cracks.

"Together you will choose one scientist," Mr. Milot says. "If you need ideas, ask me."

"Ooh, a scientist," Sophie says. "I've got an idea."

"After you research your scientist," Mr. Milot says, "you'll create a project together and present it to the class."

"Albert Einstein," Sophie whispers. "He'd be perfect."

I force a halfhearted smile. "But, Sophie, don't you think everybody already knows about him?"

"That's why he's perfect, David. We won't have to explain every little thing. We can just get to the good stuff."

"But wouldn't it—"

Sophie touches my arm. My *arm!*

Her touch is to me what Kryptonite is to Superman. "Albert Einstein's a great choice," I say.

Mr. Milot hands out instructions about the project.

Names _____
Name of your APPROVED scientist

_____

Once you've done research from at least THREE sources, you may choose one of the following projects to present to the class:

   One: Write a play that includes your scientist as the main character. The play must explain why s/he is important and what major contributions s/he has made.

   Two: Create a board game, using information about your scientist. You will need to explain your choices and demonstrate how playing the game will teach students about your chosen scientist.

   Three: Create a picture book of at least ten pages, using art and words to teach others about your chosen scientist.

Four: Produce a three- to five-minute video that introduces your classmates to the achievements of your chosen scientist.

Most importantly, work hard together and HAVE FUN!

I stare at number four. I can't believe that Mr. Milot is letting us do number four. It's like he's offering me—I mean us—an A.

Sophie taps the paper and leans close. "We *have* to do the second one."

"Huh?"

"When Mom was homeschooling me, I made this awesome board game to learn Spanish."

"Cool," I say, but inside I'm panicked. *No way we're doing a stinkin' board game when we can shoot a video.*

"I'll show it to you sometime," Sophie says.

"Cool," I say again, but I'm thinking, *I'll show you the videos I've made and you'll want to pick number four. At least, I hope you do.*

Sophie touches my arm again with her Kryptonite fingers.

Stay. Strong. Must. Choose. Video.

"We could even start making the game today." Sophie looks at me with those green eyes. "If you want to."

She lifts her hand from my arm, and the spell is broken.

"Must. Choose. Video."

"What?" Sophie says, and looks at me like I have slugs crawling up my nostrils.

"Video," I say. "I think we should make a video. Number four."

Sophie waves her hand. "David, I'm hopeless with that stuff."

This time I put my hand on Sophie's arm and feel goose bumps on her skin. "I'll teach you."

Having my fingers on her arm works like Kryptonite on her, too, because she says, "Okay. If you show me how."

Some kid is talking to Mr. Milot at his desk.

I lean close to Sophie. "If you want to come over after school, I'll show you some of the videos I've already made." *Did I just say that? What if Sophie thinks they're lame, like Tommy Murphy does?*

"Cool," Sophie says. "Let me get our scientist approved."

Sophie writes *Albert Einstein* on our paper, rushes to Mr. Milot's desk and comes back with his signature in red ink. "All set," she says.

When the buzzer sounds, I barely have time to pick up my notebook before Sophie pulls me—*pulls me!*—down the halls and out the doors of Harman Middle School.

22

Sophie leans into the passenger window of a silver Prius. "Mom, this is my friend David." She pushes me in front of the window.

"Hello, Ms. Meyers."

"We need to work on a science project, and David invited me over to his house."

A few cars pull around Sophie's mom's car.

"Well, I—"

Mr. Carp marches forward. He taps on the hood of Ms. Meyers's car. "Move along, please," he says through his megaphone.

I turn my back to Mr. Carp. All I need is for him to say, "Hi, Mr. Greenberg. Glad to see you back from suspension."

That's why when Sophie opens the back door and pushes me into the car, I don't resist. I also don't resist because, well, Sophie Meyers pushes me into the backseat of the car.

As Ms. Meyers pulls out, I look back and see Elliott and Tommy walking away from school. Together. Tommy's way taller, and Elliott hangs back a little, like he doesn't quite belong beside Tommy. I'm just glad to be in this car and driving away from them.

"My gosh. It's like a zoo," Ms. Meyers says. "I came an hour early to avoid this kind of thing."

"An hour early?" Sophie says.

"Well, I thought . . ." Her mother doesn't finish.

I shrug, like I can't believe her mother would do something so lame, but inside I feel a pang, because Sophie's mom not only picked her up from school but cared enough to be the first car in line.

"So, David," Ms. Meyers says, looking in the rearview mirror, "where do you live? And what is this science project, anyway?"

"It's cool, Mom," Sophie says. "We can make a picture book or whatever about a scientist. And we picked Albert Einstein."

"But we're going to make a video," I say before giving Ms. Meyers directions to our house.

Ms. Meyers pulls into the driveway behind Dad's car. "I'll just come in for a minute." She glances into the review mirror. "To meet your mom."

Why do people always assume?

"Or does she work? Because I don't allow Sophie to go over to someone's home without parental supervision."

"I'm sure my dad's home, Ms. Meyers. He works from home."

"Oh. What does he do?"

Sophie rolls her eyes. "Mom."

"I'm just curious, honey."

"He's a newspaper writer." I'm not allowed to say he's Alan of

"Alan's Answers" or, Dad says, it would destroy his anonymity. Whatever the heck that means.

"Oh, that's interesting," Ms. Meyers says.

Not really. He sits in his office and stares at his computer most of the time.

"I read the *Bucks County Courier Times* cover to cover every day."

"Mom!"

"It's true, Sophie. That's what I do after you leave for school. And my favorite column is that "Alan's Answers." I love how he tells it like it is."

Sweat breaks out on my upper lip, and since there are no mustache hairs there to catch it, salty droplets drip into my mouth. Sweat erupts from my bacteria-laden armpits, too. *If I don't get out of this car soon, I'll drown in my own sweat!*

"Mom!" Sophie screams, and opens her car door.

The cool air instantly dries my sweat.

"We have a project to do. Come on, David." Sophie yanks me out of the car and pulls me toward my house.

Ms. Meyers follows.

"Dad, we're home," I yell, hoping he doesn't come out of his office dressed in penguin boxer shorts or something else totally embarrassing.

"Be right there," he calls from his office.

Ms. Meyers stands in our foyer and wrings her hands, as if she's about to meet someone important, like Jon Stewart. *It's just my dad*, I want to say.

"Who do we have here?" Dad asks, walking toward us, wearing jeans and a T-shirt. He looks at Sophie. "You're definitely not Elliott."

Sophie tilts her head. "Uh, no. I'm Sophie," she says, thrusting her hand toward Dad.

"Hi, Sophie." Dad shakes her hand.

"And I'm Ms. Meyers."

"Glad to meet you," Dad says.

"Your son says you write."

Dad shoots me a stern look.

"Yup, I told her you write articles for the paper."

"Ah, yes," Dad says. "Articles. Come in."

Sophie pulls on my pinky finger.

"Well, we need to go up and work on our science project," I say.

"Okay," Dad says as Sophie and I charge upstairs.

I hear Dad offer Ms. Meyers a cup of coffee.

She stammers. "I—I'd . . . love to, but don't want to keep you from your work."

"I'm done for the day," Dad says.

Atop the stairs, Sophie says, "Is she annoying or what?"

I shrug, thinking about how Mom used to read Elliott's aura or talk about his energy field when he came over. Elliott and I would laugh about it later, but it was embarrassing, especially the time Mom told him he was Julius Caesar's bodyguard in a past life. "Your mom seems okay," I say.

I think I'm taking Sophie to my room to show her one of my *TalkTime* videos, but I detour instead to Lindsay's door. I know I'm here to show off Sophie. "My sister's room," I say, and knock.

Just as Lindsay yells, "Enter," I remember that she might have zit-be-gone cream slathered all over her face.

"Maybe we should go to my room instead."

"Come in!" Lindsay yells in a ferocious voice.

I crack the door open. "Hey, Linds, you busy?"

She swivels around from her computer. "Of course I'm busy, moron. I'm in high school now." Her face is zit cream free.

I sigh and open the door all the way to let Sophie in.

"Oh, hi," Lindsay says. "You're not Elliott."

What is it with people?

"This is Sophie. She came over to work on a project."

"Hey, Sophie."

When Sophie wanders to Lindsay's CD rack, I'm afraid my sister's going to yell at her to get away from her stuff, but she doesn't. Instead, she gives me two thumbs up.

My neck gets warm.

"You like Ben Harper?" Lindsay asks.

Sophie shrugs. "My mom makes me listen to classical CDs. I wish I had a collection like this."

"I can burn anything you like," Lindsay offers.

"Really?"

"Definitely."

Thank you, Lindsay Melanie Greenberg, for being nice to Sophie. And for not having zit-be-gone cream on your face.

I pull my shoulders back. "We're heading to Bubbe's now."

"Good luck," Lindsay says, and flops onto her bed.

When we're out of the room, Sophie whispers, "I like your sister."

"She's okay. Sometimes."

Downstairs, Ms. Meyers is still chatting with Dad, so I grab Sophie's elbow, and we duck past the kitchen and head to Bubbe's apartment.

Sophie's peppermint whisper on my ear surprises me. "What's a Bubbe?"

I lean close. "Yiddish word for 'grandmother.' "

"Oh," Sophie says as Bubbe's door swings open. Her apartment smells like cinnamon.

"Bubbe, this is Sophie, one of my friends from school."

Bubbe takes Sophie's cheeks in her wrinkly palms. "I'm so glad to meet one of David's little friends."

"Uh, Bubbe," I say, pulling Sophie out of her clutches, "we stopped by to say hi, but have to head up to my studio now."

"Oh. Your studio." Bubbe pretends to grab onto lapels and struts around her living room. "Even a big-shot star needs to eat." Bubbe winks at Sophie, grabs our hands and guides us to the table in her tiny kitchen. "You can go to your studio after you nosh on a little Jewish apple cake. Just baked."

Sophie stares at Bubbe with wide eyes, and I can't tell if she likes Bubbe or is overwhelmed.

"Eat, *bubelahs*!" Bubbe says, sliding plates of cake in front of us, along with glasses of soy milk.

I hope Sophie doesn't think soy milk is weird.

Bubbe watches us eat. Every bite. You can't refuse Bubbe. A Jewish grandmother trying to feed you is more persuasive than the heads of the Mafia, the CIA and the FBI combined.

"It's delicious," Sophie says about twenty-seven times. "May I have the recipe?"

I know she's just kissing up, but it makes Bubbe glow. "Of course, *sheyn ponem*."

Sophie tilts her head.

"Tell you later," I whisper.

The minute Sophie enters my room, she zooms to Hammy's cage, opens the lid and cups Hammy in her hands. "Mom won't let me have pets," Sophie says, nuzzling Hammy's fur. "Too many germs. Too much trouble. Allergies. Shedding. Blah. Blah. Blah."

Sophie kisses Hammy on top of his head. "You are the cutest thing ever," she coos to him. "You don't have any bad germs, do you?"

Lucky hamster!

I walk over and pet Hammy with my fingertip. "Now you've met the whole family. This is Hammy the—"

Sophie lets out a peel-the-wallpaper-off-the-walls shriek.

Before I can restart my heart and ask what's wrong, Sophie's mom bursts through the door.

How'd she get up here so fast?

"What?" Ms. Meyers's eyes are the size of matzo balls.

She rushes to Sophie and flings her arms around her shoulders. "Oh, thank goodness I hadn't left yet. What's—" That's when Ms. Meyers notices Hammy in Sophie's hands and leaps backward.

Sophie cracks up, holding Hammy way out in front of her.

"What's going on?" Dad asks, stepping into the room.

"Yeah, what's going on?" Lindsay asks, pushing past Dad.

Sophie offers Hammy up like a gift. "He . . . he . . . peed on me." She bursts out laughing again.

Lindsay laughs, too, then me, then Dad. It's contagious, but Ms. Meyers doesn't catch it. She rummages through her purse with a vengeance and thrusts a container of antibacterial liquid at Sophie. "Here."

Sophie takes the bottle.

I put Hammy back into his cage and lead Sophie to the bathroom to wash her hands. When we return, Dad is scrubbing the carpet with an old washcloth, and Sophie gives the antibacterial stuff back to her mom, who retrieves it with a tissue.

"Sophie, are you ready to go?"

"Mom," she says, "I just got here."

"Well . . ." Ms. Meyers looks at Hammy.

"She's welcome to stay for dinner," Dad says.

"Yeah," Lindsay says, secretly winking at me. "Bubbe cooks great dinners."

Ms. Meyers looks at each of us as though she's deciding if we're serial killers. Then she looks at Sophie, who is nodding like crazy. "I guess that'll be okay. I do have to run a few errands. How about if I pick you up at"—she looks at her watch—"seven-thirty?"

"Yes," Sophie says.

Her mother comes over and whispers something in her ear.

"I won't touch the hamster," Sophie says.

24

After Ms. Meyers leaves, Sophie says, "She probably stayed all that time to make sure I was okay." Sophie shakes her head. "Maybe she was afraid I'd be mauled to death by your hamster."

My treacherous hamster is buried under wood shavings, asleep. "Yeah," I say, "Hammy's pretty dangerous. He's also sort of famous."

"What?"

"He's on YouTube. I'll show you."

At the computer, I pull up our *Hammy Time* video on YouTube. "I made this one with my friend Elliott," I say, that familiar ache in my stomach. "It was right after I got Hammy."

In the video, Hammy's up on his hind legs, and Elliott and I edited it to make it look like he's holding a microphone and singing while that old song "U Can't Touch This" plays in the background. We dubbed in Elliott's voice to make it say "Hammy time" instead of "Hammer time."

"Oh my gosh," Sophie says, wiping tears of laughter from her eyes. "That's so cute. Play it again."

Sophie watches the video six more times. "Why don't you have more views and comments?" she asks. "This is too funny to have only four comments."

"We never told too many people." I think of Tommy Murphy's words. "Besides, our videos are kind of lame."

"Lame!" Sophie says. "You mean hilarious." She leans next to me and takes over the keyboard.

"What are you—"

"I'm sending the link to my e-mail address. Did you make other ones?"

I'm afraid she'll think I'm a giant dork, but I hold my breath and show her the *TalkTime* video I made with Magazine Cover Jon Stewart.

Sophie laughs in all the right places and sends that link to her e-mail address, too.

"I love your Top Six and a Half list, David. Does your sister know about—"

"No," I say. "Or I don't think I'd be here right now."

"Gotcha," Sophie says. "I can't believe you don't have like a million views."

I feel heat creep up my neck.

"I'm going to send the links to my homeschool network."

"Your what?"

Sophie pushes hair out of her face. "You know, a network of other kids who are homeschooled."

"How many is that?"

She leans back. "In the United States or internationally?"

My eyes widen.

"It's pretty big."

My first thought is that I want to tell Elliott that all these homeschooled kids will be watching our videos, but then I remember. Elliott and I aren't friends anymore. He made that mean joke about my mom today. And I said something just as mean about his dad. *How have things gotten like this between us?*

"You okay?" Sophie asks.

I nod, even though I'm not.

She points to one of the comments for the video. "Who's Matzo Ball Mama?"

I nod toward downstairs. "Bubbe."

Sophie laughs and covers her mouth. "That explains what she wrote: 'Excellent video, but lose the bit about your sister, mister!'"

"That's what I get for showing her how to use YouTube."

"Who's LADM?" Sophie asks, pointing to the screen. "He wrote, 'Two thumbs up. If you see only one video this year, make it this one.'"

"No clue," I say, "but he writes really nice comments on our videos."

"Cool. A mystery fan. I'm totally going to let my friends know about this."

"Thanks."

"You should be on WHMS in the morning, David." She waves her hand. "You know, reading the school news."

I sit taller. "You think?"

"You'd be great."

"I don't even know where the TV studio is at Harman." My stupid voice cracks. *What if I was on WHMS and my voice cracked with the whole school watching?*

"I think it's in the media center. When I went today during lunch, I saw a door that said 'WHMS News' on it."

Sophie is leaning back on my bed, her curly hair swinging loosely.

I inhale a faint whiff of peppermint.

"David?"

"Yes?"

"We'd better get started."

"Oh, right." I type the Web address for Wikipedia.

By the time Bubbe calls us for dinner, we have three pages of notes about Albert Einstein.

"I didn't know some of this stuff," I say. "He *was* pretty amazing."

"See?" Sophie says. "Einstein was the perfect choice, right?"

I look at Sophie hunched over her notebook, curly red hair framing her face.

"Yeah." I let out a long, slow breath. "Perfect."

25

Bubbe carries a plate of sweet-smelling blintzes into the dining room. My stomach rumbles. Lindsay follows with a dish of sour cream, and Dad's got a salad in one hand and dressing in the other. We take our places at the table, but there's an empty seat. *Mom's old seat.*

"Where's Sophie?" Lindsay asks.

"She was right behind me." Feeling awkward about losing my guest on her first visit, I call from the dining room, "Sophie?"

From the living room comes a deep, throaty horn blast.

Dad's fork slips from his fingers and clatters to the table.

Bubbe's hand goes to her mouth.

And Lindsay looks at me with her jaw dangling. She's the first to move; then we all rush toward the living room.

Sophie stands between the TV and the coffee table, holding Mom's tuba—*Mom's tuba!*—with air squirreled in her cheeks for her second blow.

Don't!

She blows with gusto, and a loud blast comes from the bowels of the tuba.

A tiny noise escapes Dad's throat.

The last time we heard that tuba was about two years ago in the middle of the night. It wasn't the sounds from the tuba that woke me, though. It was my parents' screaming at each other.

"Anita, you can't play the tuba in the middle of the night. You'll wake the kids."

Lindsay and I crouched on the top step, held hands and listened.

"You don't let me do anything, Alan," Mom shrieked. "Anything at all."

"If by 'anything' you mean stopping you from buying those damn figurines by the armful while we're going broke, then yeah, Anita, I don't let you do anything. Or holding séances when Lindsay brings her girlfriends over. Yeah, I kind of frown on that, too."

"I'm suffocating here," Mom shrieked. "Suffocating!"

Lindsay squeezed my hand so tight it hurt.

There was silence; then Mom wailed, "Alan, I can't—"

"It'll be okay, Anita," Dad said softly. "It'll be okay."

A few days later, Mom left.

Sophie moves the tuba from her lips and bursts out giggling.

When she's met with stone silence, she puts the tuba back in the corner, wipes her lips with the back of her hand and says, "Sorry. Mom taught me how to play the trumpet. I just thought . . ."

Her voice trails off.

Bubbe looks at Dad's fallen face and rushes to Sophie. "That was lovely, Sophie. Just lovely." Bubbe guides Sophie past us, into the dining room. "But dinner's getting cold," she says. "And it's a shame to eat my blintzes cold. Wait till you taste them. Lots of sweet cheese and blueberries."

When nobody says anything while we eat, Sophie nudges me with her foot under the table.

"So," I say. "We found out one very interesting fact about Einstein."

"That he was way smarter than you?" Lindsay says.

Bubbe shoots Lindsay a look.

"No," I say. "Well, yes, but . . . he was an Ashkenazi Jew."

"We're Ashkenazi Jews," Bubbe says. "Your *zeyde*—God rest his soul—and I were both from eastern Russia."

"Wait a second." I run to the kitchen to get paper and a pencil.

"Where were you from again?"

"Eastern Russia," Bubbe says, her cheeks stuffed with blintze. "Why?"

"School assignment."

"Oh," Sophie says. "I had to do that, too. But ours was due today."

My blintze goes down hard. "Yeah, we, um . . . So, Dad, where were Mom's parents from?"

Dad parks his fork midway between plate and mouth. "Hmmm. I think her mother was from Austria."

"Like Arnold Schwarzenegger," Sophie says.

"Yes, like Arnold Schwarzenegger. I can't remember where

her father's from." Dad shakes his head. "It's sad they died so young."

"David," Lindsay says, stabbing her blintze with her fork, "why don't you call and ask Mom? Oh, that's right. You can't. She doesn't have a—"

"That's enough!" Dad says.

I glare at Lindsay but go back to eating.

No one says another word the rest of the meal.

"Your family's quiet when they eat," Sophie says as we stand by the door, waiting for her mom to arrive.

I can't tell her the truth—that remembering Mom has a way of doing that to us. It's been two years now, and sometimes I wonder if it'll ever get easier.

"Yeah." I shrug. "They're kind of weird about that." *Shut up, David.* "Afraid of choking or something." *Really, shut up.* "I choked on a nickel when I was little." *Oh my gosh! Shut up!*

"Really?"

"Yeah, I saved it in a jar in my closet."

"Oh."

"It's sort of green now." *Please strike me dead. SHUT UP!*

Sophie's mom runs up our steps at exactly 7:29, holding a plastic bag out to Sophie. "Look what I found."

Sophie pulls out a paperback book with Einstein on the cover.

"Ta-dah!" Ms. Meyers says. "For your project."

"*The New Quotable Einstein?*" Sophie says. "You bought us a book about Einstein? We can do our project by ourselves, Mom."

Ms. Meyers looks down. "I just thought . . ."

I take the book from Sophie. "This is great, Ms. Meyers," I say quietly. "It will be real helpful for our project."

But Sophie still looks upset. "Let's go," she says, storming down the steps.

Ms. Meyers looks at me awkwardly. "Thanks for having Sophie for dinner."

"No problem," I say.

"I can thank him myself," Sophie yells. She gives me a quick salute, gets in the car and slams the door.

After they leave, I head to my room and glance through the book Sophie's mom bought us. Even though it seemed to make Sophie mad, there are some great quotes. I mark off the ones I think would work well in our video, then go to my closet and pull out the box of letters from Mom. *Sophie, you have no idea how lucky you are.*

I pull a piece of paper and a pen from a drawer in my desk.

Dear Mom,

I want to write to Mom about Sophie and our project, maybe even mention how Sophie's not so nice to her mom.

But all I end up writing is

Where was your father born? It's for a school assignment.
Love you,
David

I know if she answers, it will be too late for the assignment, but I want to know anyway. It feels like I lost so much after Mom left. I don't want to lose my history, too. A person should be able to find out where he came from.

I address and stamp the letter, then say good night to Hammy. Before getting into bed, I switch off the ringer on the phone in case Elliott or Tommy gets any more brilliant early-morning ideas.

I need a good night's sleep tonight.

26

In the morning, Dad is in the living room, sitting near Mom's tuba.

"Hey," I say.

When he turns toward me, I see that his eyes are red-rimmed. "How ya doing, champ?"

I know he was sitting here thinking about Mom. I wonder if he's thinking about the last time she played that tuba, and I wonder if it makes him as sad as it made me. Probably.

I nod toward the tuba. "How *you* doing?"

"Been better."

I give Dad a sympathetic look. He doesn't usually admit stuff like that.

"Hey, maybe—"

"Don't worry. Your old dad's gonna be fine."

"I know," I say, but I don't, because Dad still gets really sad sometimes.

"By the way," he says, walking into the kitchen, "what's this?" He presses "play" on the answering machine.

"It's Underwear Day at Harman," Elliott says in this real excited voice. "Don't forget to wear your Superman Underoos."

Dad presses "stop," and I slump in a chair.

"David?"

I sigh. "Things got weird between me and Elliott."

"Weird how?" Dad sits beside me and puts a hand on my knee. Everything about Elliott spills out.

Dad listens and nods. When I'm done, he waits awhile, then says, "That explains the fight." He runs a hand through his hair. "Look, David, things like this happen at your age. You'll probably make up and forget all about it."

"I don't think so," I say. "Things are pretty bad."

"You'll be surprised." Dad gets up and measures ground coffee into the filter and slips it into the coffeemaker. "Things have a way of working themselves out."

"Yeah," I say.

"Really, David. Give it time."

I know Dad's wrong. Just because he has a column where he has all the answers, it doesn't mean his answers are always right. "Things don't always work themselves out."

"Huh?" Dad says, turning from the coffeemaker.

"Some things don't work out," I say. "No matter how much time you give it."

We both know I'm talking about Mom.

27

At school, I rush to the media center.

It's a big room with tables and bookshelves, an alcove of computers and a colorful couch in front of a rack of magazines. I take a few steps inside and spot the door off to the side marked WHMS NEWS.

I hold my breath and push open the door.

Behind a glass window is the studio. In it, a woman leans over a table where a girl sits. It's Ellen Winser. A camera faces them.

"Can I help you?" says a deep voice.

I turn and see an amazing set of equipment. There's a sound board and a machine that makes the words on the screen and a TV with—

"Yo?"

Sitting behind the equipment is the heavy kid who wore a T-shirt the first day of school. He swivels in his chair to face me.

He's now wearing a T-shirt that says "I'm hungry and you're in my way."

"You need Ms. Petroccia?" he asks.

"Huh?"

"You here to see the librarian? 'Cause she's in the studio now, and—"

A loud buzz pierces through his words, and I picture Ms. Lovely shutting the classroom door with one seat at the front of the room empty. My stomach plunges.

"Uh, I was wondering if I could—"

"Spit it out, kid. I gotta get this going." He runs his hand over the equipment.

"I was wondering"—I swallow hard—"if I could work on the news."

He looks me up and down. "Sixth grader?"

I nod.

"No sixth graders," he says, and goes back to the sound board.

"But—"

Ms. Petroccia comes into the equipment room. "The media center's closed now," she says.

"Kid wants to join the news crew," the heavy boy says without looking up.

Ms. Petroccia peers at me over her glasses. "You're a sixth grader, right?"

Is it that obvious? "Yes, but—"

"No sixth graders," she says. "Sorry."

The heavy kid looks at Ellen Winser, holds up five fingers, then four, then three, then two, then points toward Ellen.

"Welcome to WHMS news. I'm Ellen Winser. Please stand tall for the pledge."

The screen in front of the boy switches to an image of a flag, and Ms. Petroccia smiles.

"Thanks anyway," I say to no one in particular and leave.

I get a heavy feeling in my stomach as I walk through the deserted halls. The pledge drifts out of each classroom I pass, then club notices. Before opening the door to Ms. Lovely's room, I pause and take a deep breath.

I go in just as Ellen Winser is announcing today's lunch menu and Ms. Lovely is turning off the TV.

28

"Mr. Greenberg," Ms. Lovely says. "You're late."

"I was in the media center," I say as I slide into my seat.

"Where is your late pass, Mr. Greenberg?"

"My . . . ?"

"Without a pass, you're late. And when you are late to my class, you get a detention."

Tommy Murphy snickers.

"Mr. Murphy," Ms. Lovely says, "would you like *another* detention?"

Tommy shuts up.

I've never gotten a detention in my life. Honor roll breakfast. Lunch with the principal for perfect attendance. But a detention? "Ms. Lovely, I can't—"

"You can't believe that in only the first week of school, you've broken dress code and come to my class late? Well, Mr. Greenberg, neither can I."

I sink way down in my seat, too embarrassed to look at Sophie. *It was her idea to go to the TV studio.*

Ms. Lovely slaps a piece of paper onto my desk. "Now, if you don't mind, I'm going to teach."

29

In the cafeteria line, I let a guy in front of me while I think about the TV studio. Besides all the great equipment the boy was running, there was a teleprompter near one of the cameras. A *teleprompter!* Those things cost a fortune.

Some kids dream about getting an NBA contract or singing on *American Idol.* I imagine sitting in front of a camera, reading from a teleprompter, just like Jon Stewart.

But I'm not going to get to do it because I'm only a lowly sixth grader!

After the lunch lady plops a few fish sticks and french fries onto my tray, I walk into the lunchroom and don't stop at Gavin's table. It's full. But before I make it to the table in the back, Tommy yells, "Yo, David, come sit with us."

When I turn in that direction, a flying object hits me square in the forehead.

"Bull's-eye!" Tommy yells.

How does he do that?

The guys at his table crack up and high-five him. Including Elliott. *Traitor!*

I expect more from Elliott. I expect him to remember when Tommy clocked him with that rock and I stood beside him while his mom glued his skin together. I expect some compassion as I stand in the middle of the lunchroom—*the middle of the lunchroom!*—with an orange at my feet, but Elliott just shakes his head and laughs, like all the other Neanderthals at the table.

I hunch my shoulders, kick the orange out of my way and slink to the table in the back. When I sit, three kids keep eating and don't even look up at me. One boy nods, then goes back to his food. And a girl lowers her book—*A Crooked Kind of Perfect*—looks at me, then puts the book in front of her face again.

I haven't felt this lonely since the day Mom left. I choke down dried-out fish sticks and oil-soaked french fries, expecting to be hit in the head by another airborne piece of fruit at any moment, but I'm not.

When the buzzer blasts, I'm relieved. Made it through another miserable lunch period. Only 177 more to go until summer break.

As I watch the Neanderthals leave, I shoot death rays at their backs. Someday I'll be a famous talk show host, and the only way they'll appear on TV is in police mug shots on the six o'clock news!

30

When I hand my assignment to Ms. Daniels in world cultures, I feel like I'm cheating, because I don't have the space filled in for Mom's father's birthplace. Or maybe I feel like I've been cheated.

In science, Mr. Milot tells me twice to stop talking to Sophie, then moves my seat for the rest of the period. Embarrassing!

At the end of the day, someone slams me into a bay of lockers. There's a mass of kids, so I can't see who did it, but I'm pretty sure I hear Tommy's obnoxious laughter as I rub my shoulder and walk out into the courtyard.

Friday at school is no better. I end the day getting shoved into the lockers. Again. Going home, I think about my rotten day and realize that the only thing that will make it better is a fat slice of Bubbe's Jewish apple cake and a cold glass of soy milk.

I run the rest of the way home.

31

On my way upstairs to say hi to Hammy and change into comfortable clothes, Lindsay bumps into me.

"Watch out," I say.

She stops. "What's with you?"

I shrug, realizing I'm thinking about Tommy's slamming me into the lockers and how much my shoulder still hurts. "Where you going?"

"Out," Lindsay says.

"Out where?"

Lindsay points downstairs. "Anywhere that's not here. It's Rock Band night."

"Nooooo."

"Yeah," Lindsay says, trotting down the rest of the stairs and out the front door.

Every few weeks, Dad and two of his buddies, Alan Wexler

and Alan Drummond, play the video game Rock Band with toy plastic guitars and drums. They're hopeless at it, and it's totally embarrassing to watch. I don't know why Dad doesn't play his real guitar. Mom said he was better than Eric Clapton, whoever the heck that is. She said she used to watch Dad all the time when he played in his college band, Widow's Kiss. Dad said she was the most loyal of all his groupies. I hope he was joking about having groupies.

Sometimes I wonder whether Mom might still be around if Dad had kept playing guitar—if he hadn't lost that part of himself. But I know that it goes way beyond Dad's not playing his guitar anymore.

I change into a T-shirt and shorts, pet Hammy behind the ears and head to Bubbe's apartment. Maybe after a slice of cake we could go to the movies and then to Rita's for a custard and a soft pretzel. Or anywhere until the two Alans leave.

"Hi, Bubbe," I say, strolling into her apartment.

Bubbe shoves keys and a fat wallet into her pocketbook. "Hi, *bubelah*. I'm late."

"For what?" I hope she'll ditch her plans and take me out instead.

"There's an interfaith peace activist meeting in town."

"An interfaith . . . huh?"

Bubbe shoulders her huge bag, and I think it's going to knock her over, but she steadies herself and puts my cheeks between her warm hands. It's like she's got portable heaters in her palms. "I've got to go," she says. "Stay here and watch TV if you'd like."

The moment she leaves, I call after her, "But what'll I eat for dinner?" thinking that might be enough to guilt her into staying home.

Bubbe appears in the doorway, breathless. "David Todd Greenberg," she says. "There's a slab of kugel in the fridge. Think you can handle the microwave?"

Before I answer, she's gone.

I turn off the light in her apartment, close the door and trudge to the kitchen.

The three Alans are in the living room, plugging in their "instruments."

Dad spots me and waves. "Join us," he calls, dangling the toy plastic microphone.

"No thanks."

"We could use you," Alan Drummond says, adjusting his guitar strap and looking very serious.

It's a toy, I want to yell. *A video game. For kids!*

"Can't," I call. "Homework."

"Hey, David," Alan Wexler says. "Watch this." He twirls one of his drumsticks. It falls out of his hand and plops noiselessly onto the carpet.

I nod, then grab the slab of kugel from the fridge and run upstairs.

"It's just you and me tonight," I tell Hammy.

Even Hammy burrows in his wood shavings and ignores me.

I take one bite of kugel, then go to my closet to get my K'nex set. When I remember I tossed it, my shoulders slump.

I turn on the computer, watch a few video clips on the *Daily Show* site and eat some more kugel. Then I check my Jon Stewart

TalkTime video on YouTube. A piece of kugel drops out of my mouth and falls onto the keyboard.

There are nearly a thousand views and forty-seven comments! *Forty-seven comments!*

I scroll through some of them while I pick kugel off my keyboard.

Great vid, dude. Make more.

2 Funny!

This rox!

"Oh my gosh," I say to Hammy. "I'm famous." I click on the *Hammy Time* video and find that it has more than fifteen hundred views and one hundred and five comments. I push my chair back. "Come on!"

I hit "refresh." One hundred and six comments. "Oh, my . . ." I press my face to Hammy's cage. "You're more famous."

Hammy looks unimpressed.

"I can't believe all those people watched our videos. And commented!" I'm dying to tell Elliott, but remember the orange incident in the lunchroom today. It feels like the nice comments fill up that empty space inside me. I wonder if this is how Jon Stewart feels on the *Daily Show* set when he walks out and hears hundreds of fans in the audience scream for him.

Take that, Tommy Murphy. My videos aren't lame. You are!

I scan the comments.

Cuuuuuute hamster.

Luv the hamster.

Hammy Time sooooo awesome.

Oh my gosh. They're eating Hammy up! I need to tell

someone. But the three Alans have started playing, so no way I'm going down there. Bubbe and Lindsay are gone. Elliott's a jerk. And I don't have Sophie's e-mail address or phone number.

Sophie! Your homeschool network. How many people did you tell?

I pull out a sheet of paper and a pen.

Mom,

You will never guess what happened. I met this girl and she came over to work on this project and

I tap the pen on my desk. It will take too long to explain. Besides, Mom doesn't even have a computer, so she won't understand what I'm talking about. I don't want to write to Mom; I want to talk to her.

But I can't.

I crumple the paper and throw it away.

I hear Alan Drummond yell downstairs, "Rock on, dudes!"

It's going to be a long, long night.

32

I'm awakened Saturday morning by guitar music. Real, out-of-tune guitar music. I hear it through the penguin earmuffs I wore to bed last night so I'd be able to fall asleep while the "band" was playing. The earmuffs are too tight—and they made my ears hurt.

I shove them into the back of my underwear drawer with the penguin bathing suit, rub my ears and follow the guitar sounds to Dad's bedroom door.

Lindsay appears from her bedroom, wiping her eyes. "What the . . . ?"

I shrug.

Her hand on the doorknob, she whispers, "On three."

"One," I say.

"Two," she says.

"Three," we say at the same time, and Lindsay flings open the door.

I'm not prepared for what I see: Dad, wearing pajamas, sits on the edge of the bed, strumming his Fender Strat. The cool Fender Strat that's been in a dusty case under his bed for years.

"What? Are? You? *Doing?*" Lindsay asks, hand on her hip.

Dad looks up. "Oh, hi. Did I wake you guys?"

"Um, *yeah*," Lindsay says.

I shake my head, and Lindsay pokes my shoulder. "Yes he did, David."

Dad's finally playing his guitar, Lindsay. Don't make him feel bad about it.

"Sorry, guys." Dad puts the guitar into its case and snaps the clips.

My heart sinks.

"I was just . . ." Dad gets that sad, misty look in his eyes.

Lindsay must not notice, because she says, "I'm going back to bed. Wake me when we're normal!" Then she stomps out.

I sit on Dad's bed. "So, what's up with the . . ." I jerk my head toward the guitar case.

"The guys, they . . ."

I know he means the other two Alans from last night. The Alans he's been friends with since he was my age.

"*They* thought we should get a *real* rock band together."

I want to be supportive, but a laugh slips out. I can't help it. I'm picturing my dad and the Alans onstage with long hair and leather pants, smashing their guitars.

"I know," Dad says. "Ridiculous, right?"

Yes. But Dad hasn't seemed this excited about anything since Mom left, so I say, "No. It's an awesome idea. What would you call yourselves? Widow's Kiss?"

Dad laughs. "Nah, that was my college band's name. We'd

need something new." Dad presses his palms onto his thighs. "Alan Drummond doesn't even have drums yet. It's just a crazy idea."

I knock my shoulder into Dad's. "It's not crazy. But you'll need a name." I head toward Dad's door, pausing to nod at his guitar case. "And more practice."

Dad rakes a hand through his wild morning hair. "I'm not sure your sister would appreciate that."

I nod toward Lindsay's room. "Practice, Dad. Even if it drives Lindsay crazy." I grin. "*Especially* if it drives Lindsay crazy."

And I go to my room and write Mom a long letter about how Dad has taken up playing guitar again and how he's forming a new band. As I drop the letter into the mailbox, I'm sure this will make Mom want to come home.

At least for a visit.

33

Sunday morning, I can't concentrate in Hebrew school. I look at the cantor but think of Sophie. She found my phone number and asked me over to work on our project.

Dad drives me to her house. "Have fun."

"I will," I say, even though my stomach flops around every time I think of her soft, curly hair. I carry the bag with the Einstein book and my camera case and ring the doorbell.

Sophie answers. "Hi, David."

In the foyer, I inhale deeply. It smells like our house did when Mom lit vanilla-scented candles for her morning yoga. I remember the morning she asked Dad to join her. He laughed and said, "Not my cup of chai tea." Mom looked hurt, so I told her I'd do yoga with her, but she just shook her head and walked away. Sometimes I wonder if Mom and Dad were always so different or if they became that way through the years.

"David?" Sophie waves her hand in front of my face.

I shake my head. "Sorry."

When Sophie closes the door, I notice a label on it that reads *puerta*. On the banister along the stairs, another label reads *escaleras*. I expect a dog to trot by with the word *perro* on its back, but I remember Ms. Meyers's reaction to Hammy and know there won't be a *perro* in this house.

Ms. Meyers walks in, wiping her hands on an apron. "Hello, David."

I nod.

"The labels are a throwback from homeschooling," Sophie says, then glares at her mom.

"I'll take them down," Ms. Meyers says. "Soon."

Sophie grabs my wrist and pulls. "We'll be in my room."

Ms. Meyers opens her mouth as though she's going to say something, but doesn't.

We go up the *escaleras*, open the *puerta* to her bedroom, sit on the *sillas* and turn on her *computadora*.

Sophie yanks the label off the computer and throws it into the trash can.

"Feel better?" I ask.

"A little. Sometimes it feels like Mom's suffocating me. She totally needs to get her own life."

I can almost hear my mom shrieking, *I'm suffocating here.* My mom did get her own life, far away from us. "I know what you mean," I say to Sophie, even though I really don't. "At least you know she cares about you."

"I guess." Sophie shrugs. "But if she cared a little less, that would be good."

"Hey, can I show you something?" I ask, eager to change the subject.

"Sure."

I call up *Hammy Time* on YouTube and scroll down. There are twenty-three new comments since last night. *Twenty-three!* And three hundred sixty-five more views.

I stare at the screen, trying to picture three hundred sixty-five people, all watching my video just since yesterday. Three hundred sixty-five people! That's like the entire sixth-grade class at Harman Middle School.

"Oh my gosh." Sophie shoves me. "This thing's going viral. All I did was send it to my homeschool network." She reads some comments. "Cartooney87 says, 'Cute hamster. I have one just like it.' Redsoxnritas writes, 'You rock. Make more vids. Pls!' and Astrokid13 says, 'Ha. Ha. Ha. Hammy's hilarious.' "

"They like it," I mutter, shaking my head. "They all like it!"

We click over to the *TalkTime* show with my interview with Magazine Cover Jon Stewart. That one has fourteen more comments. *Fourteen!* And a hundred twenty-two more views.

We read through the comments, which are almost all positive. One guy even says, *You should have ur own show! I would watch u.* Reading through all these compliments makes me feel amazing, like I used to feel when I made Mom laugh, and it makes me want to make another video like crazy. Finally, Sophie twirls a curl on her finger and says, "We'd better get started on our project."

I have an irrational urge to lean over and kiss her. After all, she's the person who got all this attention for my videos. Instead, I say, "I got a great idea for our project from the book your mom got us."

I teach Sophie how to work the camera. This requires me to be incredibly close to her peppermint-smelling skin and hair, which makes it hard to concentrate. I think about Cantor Schwartz from Hebrew school. The mole on his chin has hair growing out of it. I can concentrate again.

Sophie and I shoot several segments that involve my putting baby powder in my hair to make it look white, like Einstein's. The baby powder makes me sneeze, which makes Sophie laugh. Somehow, we keep working and manage to nearly finish editing our video by the time Ms. Meyers yells, "Dinner!" And a loud bell clangs.

I look at Sophie.

"Our dinner bell is a cowbell."

"You have a dinner bell?"

Sophie bites her lip. "Weird, right?"

Yes! "No." I check my watch. "You eat kind of early, though."

When Sophie turns to me, she's got that same look in her eyes that Dad had when I found him with Mom's tuba the other morning.

"We used to eat really late," Sophie says, twirling hair around her finger again. "*Really* late." Sophie looks up at me, then down again. " 'Cause we'd wait for my dad to come home from work. Sometimes he was late." She lets out a big breath. "Sometimes . . ."

It's weird. I know I said they eat kind of early, but now that Sophie's explaining, all I want is for her to stop. I want to tell her she doesn't have to explain if it hurts. I want to tell her about Mom and the Farmer, but I don't.

"My dad ended up moving in with some lady from work." Sophie slaps her palms onto her knees and laughs. "I've never told anyone before."

Not sure what else to do, I pat her shoulder.

It must have been the right thing, because Sophie smiles. "After that, Mom decided we'd eat dinner at a *decent* hour, and ever since, we've eaten earlier and earlier and—"

"Dinner!" Ms. Meyers shouts, and clangs the bell extra loudly.

"Coming!" Sophie leans toward me and speaks softly. "Ever since Dad left, Mom's been a little"—Sophie bites her lip again— "controlling."

"Dinner!" Ms. Meyers snaps. "Come down right now."

My heart pounds. "We'd better go."

Sophie pulls up *Hammy Time* again. "Four more views, David."

We high-five, then walk down for dinner.

34

Three place settings take up most of the tiny kitchen *mesa*.

"So nice of you to attend," Ms. Meyers says, placing a bottle of salad dressing on the table. I'm surprised when there's not a label with the Spanish translation for "salad dressing" on the bottle.

Sophie does an exaggerated curtsy. *"Gracias, Madre."*

Ms. Meyers cracks a smile, and I see that Sophie knows how to work her mom. *"De nada, mi hija."*

I wait for Sophie to sit, then slide onto the chair beside her, panicked that Ms. Meyers will expect me to speak Spanish during the meal. The only words I remember from Spanish Club are "dog" (*perro*), "rooster" (*gallo*), "hamster" (*hámster*) and "Be quiet!" (*¡Cállate!*), because Señorita Rioux yelled that at least twice each meeting.

"So glad to have you here, David. You'll get to enjoy my signature salad."

"I love salad." *As long as it doesn't have cucumbers, radishes, tomatoes, green peppers or weird frizzy lettuce.*

"Great." Ms. Meyers lays her napkin in her lap, and I do the same. "And a veggie omelet. And Sophie's strawberry-rhubarb pie for dessert. She's quite a baker, our, um, my little girl." She pats Sophie's hand.

Sophie smiles but gives an eye roll as soon as her mom turns her head.

"Hope you're hungry," Ms. Meyers says, grasping the edge of the silver foil covering the salad bowl. *"Come."*

Sophie answers my puzzled look with a whispered "Eat."

I nod.

Ms. Meyers whips the foil cover off the bowl.

I take one look and feel like I'm going to vomit.

The bowl is loaded with weird frizzy lettuce, cucumbers, green peppers, mushrooms and sliced beets! And the beets are bleeding onto the rest of the salad.

While I choke down a few bites to be polite, I wonder if Mom's hands touched the beet I'm eating.

The veggie omelet is okay, but Sophie's strawberry-rhubarb pie is incredible—sweet and tart with a buttery, flaky crust. It's even better than Bubbe's Jewish apple cake.

I eat two slices, and Ms. Meyers wraps up another slice in foil for me to give Dad when he picks me up.

"How was dinner?" Dad asks when I slide into the car.

"Okay," I mumble, guiltily wiping crumbs off my lips and shoving the empty silver foil wrapper into my pocket.

35

Monday morning, I go into Dad's office to get my detention slip from Ms. Lovely signed. He tells me he's writing a response to a twelve-year-old girl who wants to get her boyfriend's name tattooed on her wrist. "What's she even doing with a boyfriend?" Dad flicks the letter. "This kind of thing reminds me how lucky I am to have you and Lindsay."

I cough.

Dad puts the letter down. "What'd you need, pal?"

I slide the detention slip across his desk.

"Oh, a field trip already?"

I say nothing as Dad reads.

"Oh."

Guess Dad's not feeling so lucky about having me right now.

"I'm not happy about this, David."

"Me neither. I was late to class because I was checking out the TV studio."

"Still, you shouldn't have been late."

Thanks for understanding. I grab the signed slip, stuff it into my pocket and trudge to school for detention.

When I open the door to room 103-B, my eyes open wide.

The students slouching at desks are all bigger than me. Of course, kindergarteners would probably be bigger than me. But here some of the guys who turn around to look at me have stubble. Stubble!

I don't belong here!

"Up front," calls a voice.

I make my way to the front of the classroom, where a teacher holds out her hand.

I wipe my sweaty palm on my pants and extend my hand to shake. "David Greenberg," I say, getting used to the drill of giving my name.

"Nice to meet you, David Greenberg," the teacher says in a snide way. She does not take my extended hand but shows me her palm again.

I slap her five.

Kids laugh, and I feel the skin on my neck tingle.

A girl from the first row stretches her sneaker out and kicks my foot. "Your detention slip," she whispers.

I nod to show her that I appreciate her telling me.

The girl mutters, "Moron."

I suck in a breath and give the teacher my signed detention slip.

"Take a seat, David Greenberg."

There's only one unoccupied desk, and the person at the desk behind it waves.

My knees turn to matzo meal.

"Take that open seat," the teacher says, pointing. "Right there."

A few kids snicker.

One doesn't. He grins.

I feel like I swallowed broken glass.

"Now," the teacher says in a low, ominous tone.

I sit, every muscle in my body tense and tight.

The kid behind me breathes loudly. His breath is hot and rotten. It makes the tiny hairs on the back of my neck bristle as his name whirls through my mind like a hurricane.

Tommy Murphy.

36

I feel like I'm on one of those nature shows—the timid gazelle sipping water from a stream, seemingly unaware of danger lurking nearby. Tommy, of course, is the huge, hungry lion. Everyone knows what happens in those shows: the gazelle makes a desperate run for it but ends up getting eviscerated.

I check my watch and drum my fingers lightly on the desk. *The gazelle stands alone in the clearing, hoping the lion doesn't notice him.*

Something bonks off the back of my head.

My body stiffens.

The lion has marked its prey.

Another bonk. This one hits my ear. Two balls of paper lie on the floor beside me. *Great. Now I'm going to get in trouble for leaving trash.*

I turn in time for a ball of paper to hit me on the cheek.

I give Tommy the fiercest look I can muster.

Tommy mouths, "Sorry."

Yeah, right. Jerk!

On Tommy's desk, there's an arsenal of paper balls.

I face front, sink low in my seat and pray that something shiny will distract him. *Why does detention last so long?*

That's when I feel the next bonk. On my neck. *Hello? Little help here.*

Another bonk. And another.

I sink so low that only my head is still above the chair. *The gazelle tries to blend in with the environment, making himself less of a target. Will the lion be fooled?*

I feel a bunch of bonks at once. Bonk. Bonk. Bonkity-bonk bonk. Bonk! Some girl laughs out loud.

I'm sure this will inspire the teacher to at least look up from the papers she's grading. It doesn't.

There are balls of paper all around my desk. Evidence! I clear my throat as though there's something stuck in it.

The gazelle makes a desperate attempt to summon help from a larger, stronger gazelle.

That's when something hard hits me on the back of the head. There's an eraser on the floor. A fat pink eraser! What's next? An electric pencil sharpener?

I clear my throat more loudly.

Tommy kicks my chair, but I don't pay attention.

The teacher glares at me. "Do you need something, David Goldberg?"

"Greenberg," I say, correcting her. "No, I'm fine."

The teacher walks over and kicks one of the paper balls. "What's all this trash around your desk?"

I shrug. *Tommy Murphy did it. Tommy Murphy. Tommy Murphy.*

"Pick it up," she says.

"Me?" I touch my chest.

She nods.

Tommy snickers.

"And you," she says, tapping on Tommy's desk, "you must love coming here, because you'll be visiting me every day for the rest of the week. Now apologize to Mr. Goldberg."

"I w-was, um . . . kidding around," Tommy stammers. "Really, we're just—"

"Apologize!" the teacher barks. "Or you'll get a month of detentions."

Tommy sinks low in his seat, shoots me a killer stare and mutters, "Sorry, Goldberg."

"Good," the teacher says, and walks back to her desk. "And that floor had better be cleaned up."

When her back is turned, Tommy slaps me on the head.

Against my better judgment, I swivel and face him.

He locks eyes with me, then slides a finger slowly across his neck.

The gazelle realizes he's in grave danger, but can't find an escape route.

I slip out of my seat and pick up the wads of paper and the eraser. I think of throwing the eraser away, but I put it on Tommy's desk instead as a peace offering. *Please don't kill me.*

Tommy throws it at my forehead. Bonk!

I take a deep breath, turn and dump the paper balls into the trash can.

By the time the bell finally buzzes and I bolt to math class, I'm sure I have a red mark in the middle of my forehead and a death threat hanging over me.

The gazelle manages to escape to safety.

Momentarily.

37

When I get home, I throw my backpack onto the floor, turn on the computer and watch a few clips from *The Daily Show*. Even though they're really funny, I don't laugh.

Lindsay opens my door and flops onto my bed. "Hey, David."

"Hey," I say, signing onto my YouTube account. "Make yourself comfy."

"I will," she says, propping my pillow under her head. "I've got a giant paper due tomorrow and I don't feel like—"

"No way!" I scream.

"What?" Lindsay rushes to me and reads the message over my shoulder. "David." She smacks the top of my head. "This guy read about your videos on the *Daily Show* forum. He said they're hilarious and you have to make more."

"Wow," I say, not really believing that someone wrote about my videos on the *Daily Show* forum.

"I guess people actually watch your videos, David. Maybe I should check them out."

"Yeah," I say. "You wouldn't believe how many—" Then I remember the Daily Acne Forecast. "I mean, there's only a small group of fans. You'd probably think the videos are lame." I shrug as though it's no big deal, but it is a big deal. I'm becoming famous on the Internet. Hundreds and hundreds of people I don't even know are watching my videos. And liking them. And posting about them on the *Daily Show* forum.

Then I think about Tommy Murphy telling me my videos are lame. I think about him sliding his finger across his throat at me in detention today. And about how completely alone I felt in the lunchroom.

How can things be going so well online when I feel like such a schmo at school?

I take a deep breath, knowing I should start my homework, but instead, I read the guy's message again and decide to do something else.

38

I set up the camera and tape fake New York to the wall behind my bed.

I bang two empty paper-towel rolls together and say, "Action."

Like Jon Stewart, I start off the show by scribbling madly on a piece of paper, then look up and say, "Welcome to *TalkTime* with David Greenberg and . . ." I almost say, *Elliott Berger*. Almost. I bang the paper-towel rolls together again. "Take two: We're . . ." I clear my throat and try again. *Darn you, Elliott!* "Take three: Welcome to *TalkTime* with David Greenberg. I'm going to do a series of shows about how to survive middle school. Today's show is about dress code. But first, our Daily Acne Forecast."

I take my camera off the tripod and knock on Lindsay's door.

"Come in," she calls, "unless you're a giant doofus."

I go in.

"David, I said unless—"

"Smile," I say, interrupting her insult, and train the camera on her face, which honestly doesn't look so bad today.

"Get out! I have to work on this paper."

On the way back to my room, I decide what I'll write to go along with the footage of her face: *Today's acne forecast: sunny with a 30 percent chance of blackheads later this week.*

Then I take my time writing the Top Six and a Half list. When I've got it pretty much the way I want it, I memorize the list and set up the camera. It's still hard to position the camera at the right height to film myself. This would be much easier if Elliott were here to help.

But he's not, so I go on.

"The Top Six and a Half Reasons to Follow Dress Code at School.

"One: If someone at school wants to beat you up, it will be hard for them to find you if you're dressed like everyone else.

"Two: It will make your parents happy. Your parents give you money when they're happy.

"Three: Because I say so." (I turn the camera to Hammy.)

"Four: The Dress Code Police can be anywhere. Anywhere!" Later, when I'm editing, I'll find a photo of a restroom door and insert it into the video here.

"Five: Just be glad *this* isn't your school's dress code." Online I found a photo of a dog dressed as a clown that I'll edit in at this part.

"Six: If your school doesn't have a dress code, where is your school? I'm transferring!

"And the most important reason to follow school dress code is . . .

"Six and one-half: It's a great way to avoid getting a detention!"

Then I put on my collared shirt, pose in front of the camera and say, "This is dress code." Next I borrow Lindsay's purple dress. *What I don't do for my career!* In front of the camera, I put my hand on my hip and say in a high-pitched voice—which is not such a stretch for me—"This is a dress, but it's *not* dress code." Then I turn off the camera, take off the dress and throw on my collared shirt with my "Be nice to me. I might be famous someday" T-shirt over it. And I stick pencils up my nostrils, turn on the camera and say, "This is snot dress code." Then I wear a collared shirt, put a different collared shirt on top of my head, dance around and say, "This is dress code. Sort of."

When I edit later, I'll insert a shot of Hammy, Photoshop khaki pants and a collared shirt on him and say, "This is dress code. Thanks, Hammy."

To wrap up, I say in my best announcer voice, "Wherever you are, kids, don't do dress code. I mean, er . . ." Suppressing a laugh, I say, "This has been *TalkTime* with David Greenberg. And now, your moment of Hammy . . ."

I crack up, knowing that this will be my best *TalkTime* yet. And if Elliott sees it, he'll wish he could have worked on it with me.

I start editing by taking the image of Hammy in the khaki pants and collared shirt and inserting a surfboard under his feet so it looks like he's surfing. On the left side of the screen, I write *Director—David Greenberg; Producer—David Greenberg; Host—David Greenberg; Guy in a Dress—Beats Me; Daily Acne Forecast—Lindsay Greenberg; Well-Dressed Hamster—Hammy Greenberg.*

I upload the video to YouTube, do my math homework and check back online. The video already has thirteen views and one comment, from Felfdom: *Cute dress, dude. UR 2 funny!!!*

I check my Magazine Cover Jon Stewart *TalkTime*. There are more than fourteen hundred views and three more positive comments.

I'm feeling dazed by how many people are watching my videos when Bubbe yells, "Come down for dinner, David. It's late."

My stomach grumbles. "Coming!" Before turning off the computer, I glance out the window. *When did it get so dark?*

I walk downstairs to the smell of Bubbe's brisket and the sound of the phone ringing.

Lindsay grabs it. "Hello? Yes, he's right here. Hold on."

Lindsay mashes the phone against her stomach. "David . . . it's for you." Her cheeks are bright pink.

"Elliott?" I mouth.

Lindsay shakes her head.

"Sophie?"

She shakes her head again.

"Tommy Murphy?" My heart stampedes.

Lindsay hands me the phone and whispers, "It's a reporter from the *Bucks County Courier Times*."

"Hello?"

A deep voice says, "David Greenberg?"

"Yes?"

"Hi, David. My editor got a call from a parent of a student at Harman Middle School about your *TalkTime* videos."

Could it have been Sophie's mom? Or Sophie pretending to be her mom?

"It seems like you're becoming quite the local Internet celebrity."

"Uh, I guess."

"Well, if it's okay with you, I'd like to talk to your mom about interviewing you for an article I'd like to write for the newspaper."

I blink a few times. "I'll get my dad."

39

I'm in bed, thinking about the questions the reporter asked today: What inspired me to create *TalkTime*? Am I a big fan of Jon Stewart? What do I want to be when I grow up? Duh! I have to ask Sophie if she knows about this.

"David!" Lindsay shrieks from the hallway.

Suddenly, my bedroom door flies open.

Lindsay stands in the doorway, her face covered with zit-be-gone cream. My instinct is to grab my camera, but one look at Lindsay's tight-lipped face tells me not to move.

She marches toward me, and I press my back against the headboard.

"Okay," she says. "I figure if a reporter interviews you, your videos must be a big deal, right?"

"Right," I squeak, wishing I could move farther away from my sister, because spit is flying from her lips.

"So when I'm done with my homework, I decide to finally check out my little brother's ultrafamous videos. Right?" She steps closer.

"Right," I barely whisper.

"And what do you think I see, David?"

"Um, my—"

"I see this!" she screeches, pointing to her face. "And your stupid Daily Acne Forecast to go along with it."

I clutch my blanket.

Lindsay sticks her face in front of mine. "David, I could kill you!"

Dad charges into the room. "Whoa. Whoa. What's going on here?"

Lindsay screams at Dad, "David put me in his stupid videos!"

Dad tilts his head.

"Like this." Lindsay points to her cream-covered face.

Dad breathes hard from his nose. "David?"

"Yeah?"

"I kept meaning to look at those videos," Dad says to himself, then locks eyes with me. "Show me."

"But—"

"Now!"

I start the video with the Magazine Cover Jon Stewart interview, hoping Dad will think it's so funny he won't get mad about the part with Lindsay's cream-covered face.

Dad doesn't laugh during the funny parts at all, and when Lindsay's face fills the screen, he makes a scary sound deep in his throat.

"See?" Lindsay screeches. "What if my friends see this? Make him take it off."

Dad makes me show him all the videos, then quietly says, "Remove them."

"I can't." My heart hammers. *I'm finally getting popular, even if it is online. I can't get rid of that.*

"You will," Dad says.

"Yeah, David." Lindsay shoves me.

"Hey!" Dad says, holding her back. "What do you mean you can't?"

"Once they're up, they're up. I can't change them. I can't remove them." I don't think this is true, but I'm counting on Dad's being too clueless about the Internet to know that.

"Yes, you can, David," Lindsay says. "And you'd better."

"No, Lindsay, I really can't." I feel my face heat up because I know I'm lying. "It's impossible."

"You're a jerk," Lindsay says, shoving me so hard my head bangs into the monitor.

"It's a joke," I say, rubbing my head. "Why are you guys making such a big deal out of this?"

"It's not a joke to me!" Lindsay storms out of my room.

"You never film someone without permission," Dad says. "You should know better."

"Okay," I say, holding up my hands. "I get it. I get it."

"No, David, I don't think you do. What if Lindsay's friends at school see that? Do you think that will be easy for her?"

"Why would her friends at school look at my videos?"

Dad shakes his head and walks out, too.

"I don't know why they're making such a big deal," I tell Hammy.

He scratches against the side of his cage.

"Lindsay's only on a tiny part of the videos anyway. And besides, they really are funny."

Hammy turns away and burrows in his wood shavings.

40

The next day, Lindsay glares when I pass her in the hallway. "Don't even look at me, David. And if you ever come near me again with that camera, I'll break it."

I slink back to my room, close the door and wait until I hear her leave for school before going downstairs for breakfast.

At the table, Dad gives me the silent treatment.

"I told you to get rid of the part with your sister," Bubbe says, making a clucking noise to let me know how disappointed she is in me.

I'm relieved to leave the house . . . until I realize that it means I'll have to deal with another day at Harman. I think of the poster I would put on the lunchroom bulletin board if I had the chance.

Harmful to students
Avoid Ms. Lovely's class

Repulsive, moldy lunchroom
Maybe high school will be better
Another day in paradise . . . not!
Never get on Tommy Murphy's bad side—
and the only side he has is bad!

In Ms. Lovely's class, I ask Sophie if she knows anything about someone calling the *Bucks County Courier Times*.

She nods so hard I think her head will fall off. She whispers, "I asked my mom to call and tell them how popular your videos are. Why?"

"Someone called and interviewed me."

Sophie squeals. "No way."

I check and see that Ms. Lovely is outside the classroom door. "Yeah, it was cool." I don't tell Sophie that Lindsay found out about the Daily Acne Forecast. No need to ruin the moment.

"David, guess what else Mom did."

Ms. Lovely is still outside the door. "What?"

"Finally took down all those stupid Spanish labels."

"Really?"

Sophie nods. "She's actually loosening up a little."

"That's great," I say, but I get that empty feeling in the pit of my stomach, the one that comes when I think about my mom. Now that Sophie mentions it, I think Mom might have loosened up too much. In fact, I think before she left us, she was starting to come apart at the seams.

A wad of paper bonks off my ear and drops to the floor.

"Oops," I hear Tommy Murphy say. "Sorry, Lameberg!"

I stare straight ahead and sink low in my seat, grateful when Ms. Lovely walks to the front of the room and tells us to do all the odd problems on page thirty-seven.

It's good to have something to take my mind off things.

41

In the kitchen, a couple of days later, the *Bucks County Courier Times* lies open on the table. There's a photo of Hammy from the *Hammy Time* video and one of me from my Jon Stewart video. Someone has drawn an arrow to me in the photo and written *JERK!*

"Way to get over things, Linds," I say, even though Lindsay has already left for school and I'm the only one in the room. After I cross out the word with black marker, I read the article and think about how the reporter didn't get what I said exactly right, but it's still pretty cool to be written about in the newspaper.

Someone I know might read it, like Aunt Sherry or Ms. Berger or even Elliott. Definitely Ms. Meyers, because she said she reads the newspaper every day. Tingles erupt on the skin on my arms and shivers run up my back. *I really am getting famous.*

In math class, Ms. Lovely says in her gravelly voice, "Nice

article about you in the newspaper, Mr. Greenberg. Very impressive."

"Very impressive," Tommy mocks from behind me.

Ms. Lovely glares at him. "Mr. Murphy, I have had enough of you." She slaps a piece of paper onto his desk. "You have a detention. And if you disturb my class again, I will send you to the assistant principal's office."

As soon as Ms. Lovely turns on the TV for WHMS news, Tommy throws a ball of paper at my head. When I bend to pick it up so I don't get in trouble for leaving trash, Tommy whispers, "Read it."

I do.

Your so ded!

Even though he can't spell, I know exactly what he means. Cousin Jack's words echo in my mind, and I can't concentrate for the rest of the period. I think I know what Tommy plans to do.

On the way to my next class, I walk past the staircase, imagine Tommy throwing some kid off it—throwing *me* off it—and know that Tommy really is going to hurt me if I let him get near me.

In my next two classes, a couple of kids and another teacher tell me they read the article about me and liked my videos, but I'm too worried about Tommy to get excited about the extra attention.

In the lunchroom, when I'm walking toward the loser table in the back, Tommy appears out of nowhere, sticks his foot out and trips me. Pizza and chocolate milk fly off my tray, and I land on the floor.

Someone shouts, "Have a good trip. See you next fall!"

Kids laugh.

I scoop everything back onto my tray and feel heat explode in my cheeks. As I'm dumping my lunch into the trash, I see Tommy aiming his cell phone at me. "Give us a smile, Lameberg. After all, you're famous right?"

I turn my back to him but can hear his laughter.

"Greenberg's videos are lame," Tommy shouts. "I've seen them all and they're lame."

"Yeah," I hear someone say.

"Totally lame," someone else says.

"Even my little sister thinks they're for babies."

I rush to the table at the back of the lunchroom and keep my head down, wishing I still had my food, because at least it would be something to distract me from this horrible, never-ending period.

42

After school, Lindsay comes into my room without knocking. She waves the newspaper at me. "Guess what happened today, David."

I think about Tommy tripping me, then taking pictures with his cell phone. I think of the never-ending lunch period. I think about kids and teachers telling me they saw the article about me, and my worrying about Tommy too much to care.

"No clue," I say.

Lindsay pokes a pink-polished fingernail into my chest. "Denny J. Michaels asked me what the weather was supposed to be like today."

I shrug, wondering why Lindsay is telling me this.

"Denny J. Michaels happens to be the cutest guy at Bensalem High, David. Anyway, I can't believe he's talking to me, a mere mortal, so I think fast and start answering him. That's when he says, 'I mean the Daily Acne Forecast.' And he and all the kids around him crack up. At me. Thanks, David!"

Lindsay throws the newspaper at my face.

"I'm s—"

But she's already gone.

43

I knock softly on Hammy's cage, but he's curled into a ball under his wood shavings. His whiskers twitch in his sleep, and he's so cute that even though I need company, I don't wake him.

I grab a piece of paper and a pen.

Dear Mom,

> **I really wish you'd come home soon.**
> **It's nice here now.**
> **Dad's playing his guitar all the time. I'm doing great in school, and things are real calm and peaceful. Even Lindsay says she misses you a lot. I think you'd be happier now.**
> **Love,**
> **David**

I read my lies, crumple the paper and toss it into the trash can.

Online I've got hundreds of new views on my videos and dozens of nice comments, which is really great, except that the people who really matter to me either are not talking to me or are yelling at me because they're mad. And all the funny videos in the world can't change that.

44

I'm glad to have made it through Friday in school, but I have a bad feeling about Tommy.

When the final buzzer sounds, I dash out of class and down the hall. I'm in the bright light of the courtyard before anyone else. Except Tommy.

"Hey, Lameberg," he says, standing in front of me and crossing his arms.

I look up at him—way up—then my eyes dart around as I look for an escape route.

"I thought you'd be out here early, so I skipped my last class."

"Oh," I hear myself say in a tight, panicked voice.

"Yeah," Tommy says. "I want to give you something."

I hold my breath and brace for the first blow.

"Take it," Tommy says.

I realize I closed my eyelids. When I open them, I see Tommy's palm extended with a slip of paper on it.

Slowly, I lift my trembling fingers and pluck the paper from Tommy's hand.

45

Inside my house, my sweaty hand still grips the paper Tommy gave me. I didn't read it in the courtyard. When I realized that Tommy wasn't going to kill me, I ran.

But now, trying to catch my breath, I wonder what's on it. *A death threat? A time and place for me to meet him over the weekend?*

I drop my backpack, run up to my room and look at the paper. There's a Web address, on it. A YouTube address.

I'm online in a flash. I call up the video. It looks like the lunchroom at Harman, but it's hard to tell because of the white arrow in the middle. I press the arrow.

I see myself on the screen, scooping up pizza and chocolate milk. I look scared. Someone says, "Have a good trip. See you next fall!" Kids crack up.

Tommy wasn't taking pictures of me with his cell phone. He was making a video.

When it's over, words appear on the screen: *David Greenberg—Lamest Kid at Harman!!!*

How did that Neanderthal know how to do that? Did Elliott help him?

I scroll down and see that twelve people viewed this video. Twelve! I can never face the kids at Harman again.

I turn off the computer and bite my lower lip.

I pace around my room, thinking of a video I could make about Tommy. I'd call it *Neanderthal at Harman*. Mine would be much better than his. It would be . . . I couldn't make a video about Tommy or he'd kill me. I wouldn't do it anyway, because it's incredibly mean. It makes a person feel exposed and violated. Even a kid as mean as Tommy Murphy doesn't deserve—

I stop pacing and walk down the hall. I knock on Lindsay's door.

"Enter unless you're David Greenberg."

I go in anyway.

Lindsay swivels around from her desk to face me.

I must have a funny expression on my face, because she says, "What's wrong? Did somebody give you an A-minus on a test?"

"I'm sorry," I barely peep.

"What?"

I look into my sister's eyes. My sister, who held my hand when Mom and Dad were screaming in the living room that night with the tuba. My sister, who let me sleep in her room for two weeks after Mom left. My sister, who I totally humiliated and embarrassed on my videos. "Lindsay," I say, "I'm sorry. I'm really, really sorry."

"Wow."

"What?"

"I think you really mean it."

I nod and walk out of her room. *How could I have done that to her?*

In my room, I go online to delete all the videos with footage of Lindsay, but when I pull up the Magazine Cover Jon Stewart video, there are 151,430 views and eighty-six comments.

I can't believe it.

And I can't delete it, either.

46

I spend much of the weekend answering messages about my videos, four of which are from fans in Australia, London, Belize and Singapore. But my heart really isn't in it. I check Tommy's lame video of me obsessively. By Sunday night, there are twenty-six more views, but I think most of them are from me.

No one, thank goodness, has commented.

As I walk to school Monday, I feel like I'm loaded down with rocks. I'm sure the minute I enter the courtyard, everyone will point and laugh.

But no one pays attention to me. They talk in groups and laugh and shove each other, but not one person even nods to acknowledge my existence. It's strange that people in Australia, London, Belize and Singapore make a fuss over me online but at my own school, I'm sort of invisible.

In the hall outside math class, Tommy stops me with a hand on my shoulder. "Did you like my video, Lameberg?"

"What video?" I say, feeling proud of myself for coming up with that.

"Look, Lameberg," he says, shoving my shoulder into the wall, "don't act stupid with me. I'm still going to get you. I owe you for making me get that week of detentions. Remember?"

I gulp, nod and slip into the classroom.

Sophie smiles at me, but I'm too shaken to smile back. I open my math book and pretend to study.

In the lunchroom, I see Elliott sitting at the Neanderthals' table. When he turns his head in my direction, I look down at my so-called food.

I thought it would get easier not hanging out with Elliott, but it actually gets harder. It's not like I have a thousand friends lined up to hang out with me. It was always me and Elliott. And now it's just me and my online fans, but they can't keep me company in the lunchroom or walk to school with me or make new *TalkTime*s with me.

The moment the buzzer signals the end of the day, I find a different door to exit from, avoid the courtyard and race home.

In my room, there's an envelope on my bed.

I see the Xs and Os over Mom's return address and inhale, expecting a whiff of her vanilla scent, but it smells like paper. Without opening the envelope, I take it to Lindsay's room.

"Enter," she yells when I knock.

Lindsay's on her bed, reading *Animal, Vegetable, Miracle*.

I wonder if she's still mad at me. I don't blame her if she is.

"Hey, David. What's up?"

She doesn't sound mad.

I dangle my envelope. "You get one, too?"

"Uh-huh."

"Open it yet?"

"Nope," Lindsay says.

"Are you going to?"

"Nope."

"But, Linds, Mom wrote that she wishes—"

"Nope!" My sister puts her book in front of her cream-covered face again. "David, did you want something?" she asks from behind the book.

I squeeze my envelope. "Nope." And I walk out. *Why does Lindsay have to be like that? Mom can't help that she has some "is-sues," as Dad calls them. I mean, it's not like Mom disappeared completely from our lives, like Elliott's dad did. At least she writes to us.*

In my room, I pet Hammy and change his water. I'm dying to know what Mom wrote, but her letters don't come every day, so I savor them. I brush my teeth, check the hair under my armpits—two new hairs!—and work my Rubik's Cube for a few frustrating minutes before tearing open the envelope.

Dear David,

My father came from Poland when he was six. Hope this arrives in time for your assignment. ☺

"Nope," I say to the letter.

I also hope the beginning of school is going well. You and El-liott must be having loads of fun together.

"Nope."

Have you made lots of new friends, too? I'll bet you have. And your teachers must love you.

I think of Ms. Lovely and shake my head. "Nope."

You've probably joined a bazillion clubs, and I'm not there to hear about any of them. Next time we're in town, I'll use the phone at the library and give you and Lindsay a call.

My heart leaps. I rush back into Lindsay's room, waving the letter. "She's going to call."

Lindsay slams her book closed. "No, David, she's not. And don't come in without knocking."

"She is," I say, and run back to my room to finish reading her letter.

I sewed your name and Lindsay's name into the new quilt I'm making. It's a good thing I've made so many quilts, because you wouldn't believe how coooold it's getting here. ☹

Well, it was a long day, and I have a wicked headache. Besides, it's getting hard to read with only a candle's dim light.

Peace and cupcakes,

Mom

I write back immediately.

Mom,

You won't believe this, but they wrote an article about me in the *Courier Times*. It's about my videos. And there's a picture of

Hammy. I know you don't have a computer . . . or even electricity—ha-ha—but I thought you'd like to read it.

I cut it out, fold it and slip it into an envelope.

I'm sorry Lindsay isn't writing to you. She's really busy with high school.

I haven't made a lot of friends yet, but there's one girl and we're working on a science project together about Albert Einstein.

Your new quilt sounds neat. I wish I could see it.

I take a deep breath and write the next part.

I miss you,
David

As I'm sealing the envelope, the phone rings.

"Hello?" I say, amazed I got to it before Lindsay picked up the other line.

There's breathing on the other end, then a familiar voice. "Watch out, Lameberg. You can hide from me, but I'm going to get you."

Click.

I pet Hammy for nearly ten minutes but can't get my heart to calm down. I hear Tommy's scary voice in my head and imagine him hoisting me over the railing at school, and me landing on the floor below, my skull cracking.

47

I do something I know will make me feel better. I set up fake New York to make another *TalkTime*, but I really wish Elliott were here to help me. If he were here, I'd definitely feel better.

I take a deep breath, turn on the camera, sit on my bed, scribble on some paper and look up, scribble some more, then do my best Jon Stewart grin. "Welcome to *TalkTime* with David Greenberg and Hammy." I'll insert footage of Hammy later, when I'm editing. "Today, in our series about surviving middle school, we'll talk about the dreaded detention. Now, on to our Top Six and a Half list."

During lunch today, I wrote and memorized my list. It wasn't like there was anything else to do.

"The Top Six and a Half Ways to Get a Detention:

"One: Dress-code violation." Later I'll insert a shot of me wearing Lindsay's purple dress.

"Two: Show up late for class.

"Three: Class? What class?

"Four: Ask for one. They're free.

"Five: Tell your teacher your hamster ate your homework." Hammy will get screen time here, munching on a tiny piece of lettuce that I hope will look like paper.

"Six: Tell your teacher your sister ate your homework." I'll insert a shot here of Lindsay eating, but this time I will get her permission first!

"And the best way to get a detention . . .

"Six and one-half: Bring your hamster to school!" Here I'll insert a picture of Hammy and use Photoshop to add a teacher standing on a chair while Hammy sits at a desk, holding a book—*Hammy Potter and the Sorcerer's Stone.*

Then I interview Ms. Tough Tomatoes, who is actually me wearing one of Mom's old wigs and a nasty scowl. And she—um, I talk about how she gives detentions for everything, including breathing too loudly or blinking too often. In the interview, Ms. Tough Tomatoes mentions the day she was so late for class that she gave *herself* a detention.

I smell Bubbe's chicken soup downstairs, so I go right into "And now, your moment of Hammy." Later, with the miracle of Photoshop, I'll insert a picture of Hammy wearing Lindsay's purple dress.

After dinner—chicken soup, baked stuffed potatoes and string beans—I edit the video, then upload it to YouTube. Five minutes after it's up—five minutes!—I have twenty-four views and two comments. JJJDAWG wrote *Funniest vid EVER!!!* and TheaterGeek wrote *You should have your own TV show! I'm posting link on* Daily Show *forum. You're freakin hilarious!*

I keep checking the stats as I put the finishing touches on the science project that's due tomorrow. When I turn off the computer for the night, I tell Hammy, "A hundred and twenty-six views and nine positive comments. We're totally famous, little dude!"

In bed, before I fall asleep, I remember the Neanderthals' table in the lunchroom today. When I walked past, every guy at the table cleared his throat and said, "Lameberg," except for one person, who sat quietly with his shoulders hunched—Elliott. He didn't say anything to me, throw anything or do anything. In fact, he looked like he didn't want to be there.

The more I think about it, the more I realize there might be a glimmer of hope that Elliott is tired of Tommy and sick of sitting at the Neanderthals' table. Maybe he even wants to be friends with me again.

There's only one way to find out.

48

Tuesday, in the lunchroom, I grip my red plastic tray and walk toward the Neanderthals' table. The strong smell of burrito and mold makes my legs wobbly.

Tommy notices me right away and says, "Hey, Lameberg," and swipes his finger across his neck.

Everyone cracks up.

My heart beats so hard it sounds like ocean waves pounding in my ears. Someone throws an empty milk carton that skims my shoulder.

I ignore it, squeeze my tray more tightly, stand right behind Elliott and say, "Hi, Elliott." My voice doesn't crack, but inside it feels like I might.

Everyone stares at me, even kids from other tables.

I stand firm, praying for Elliott to say hi back, feeling sweat drip from my armpits.

Elliott looks at Tommy, then at the other guys at the table. Finally, he turns to me and says, "Hi . . ."

My heart leaps.

". . . Lameberg."

I duck my head and walk toward the losers' table. Angry heat claws up my neck as I slam my tray down. I stab my burrito with a spork and will myself not to cry.

Not here.

Not in front of them.

49

By last period, I'm exhausted from thinking about Elliott and worrying about how Tommy will finally get me, because I know that no matter how careful I am or how fast I run, he *will* get me.

Sophie taps me on the shoulder. "Do you have it?"

I reach into my pocket and pull out the flash drive.

"Excellent."

When Mr. Milot asks for volunteers to present first, Sophie thrusts her hand into the air.

"Okay," Mr. Milot says, nodding at me and Sophie. "Show us what you've got."

I start the video, then walk back to my seat.

Sophie leans close enough that I smell peppermint.

I focus on the images of Albert Einstein that appear on the screen, but it's not easy to pay attention.

"The only thing that interferes with my learning is my education."—Einstein

And Sophie Meyers, I think, inhaling her peppermint scent. Somebody yells, "Oh, yeah!" A few kids cheer.

"Settle down," Mr. Milot says.

After that quotation comes a list of the schools Einstein attended, like the Polytechnic in Zurich, where he studied math and physics.

"Imagination is more important than knowledge. For knowledge is limited to all we now know and understand, while imagination embraces the entire world, and all there ever will be to know and understand."—Einstein

A photo of Einstein sticking out his tongue appears on the screen.

Sophie and the rest of the class, even Mr. Milot, crack up, and I feel tingles along my spine. Listening to their laughter reminds me that making videos is probably what I want to do for the rest of my life.

Einstein's major theories appear, like his theory of general relativity, which states that gravitational force is equal to the force of acceleration. That's why when a car is moving forward—force of acceleration—you feel like you're being pushed backward—gravitational force. Or why when an elevator is moving up, you feel like you're being pushed into the floor.

"You have to learn the rules of the game. And then you have to play better than anyone else."—Einstein

Einstein's honors and awards, including the Nobel Prize in Physics, scroll across the screen.

"Learn from yesterday, live for today, hope for tomorrow. The important thing is not to stop questioning."—Einstein

After that quotation vanishes, an image of me with baby powder in my hair and a fake mustache appears on the screen. Everyone laughs. On-screen, "Einstein" says, "Any questions?" while at the same time, Sophie and I hop off our stools, stand in front of the room and say, "Any questions?"

Every person in the room is silent.

It feels like a bowling ball takes residence in my stomach.

Suddenly, kids clap like crazy. Someone whistles. Another person pounds on the lab table with his palms.

Mr. Milot turns off the video. "That," he says, "is an example of A-plus work. Excellent job, you two!"

No one asks a question, but they keep clapping.

While I'm basking in the glow of an appreciative audience, Sophie puts her hands on my shoulder, leans over and kisses me on the cheek. "Thanks, David."

The rest of the world falls away.

I guess I walked back to my seat, watched other kids' presentations and probably even applauded, but I don't remember. I suppose Mr. Milot handed my flash drive back, because it's in my pocket. I can't tell you if we got homework or even if there was a fire drill.

There's only one thing I can tell you with absolute certainty: *Sophie Meyers kissed me!*

50

I'm so dazed by that tingly butterfly kiss on my cheek that I completely forget about Tommy Murphy. I'm in a crowd of kids in the courtyard when I hear, "There he is!"

I look up and see Tommy and another guy pointing and threading their way toward me.

I take off running. I don't wait for the crossing guard to signal me. I run through the intersection and hear the blast of her angry whistle. I don't look back. I just run like my butt's on fire.

By the time I jam my key into the lock on our front door, my lungs burn, and I feel like I'm going to vomit. I drop my backpack, let out a big breath and head toward the kitchen.

"David?"

I turn. Dad, Bubbe and Lindsay are in the living room. And so is some man I don't recognize.

My heart hammers. *Did something happen to Mom?*

I walk in, and the man, his brown beard neatly trimmed, smiles at me.

Do I know you?

"David," Dad says again, "this is Mr. Levine. He's a reporter from the *Philadelphia Inquirer,* and he's here to interview you."

"Me?" I touch my chest. I'm still breathing hard and wondering what Tommy and that other kid had planned to do if they caught me.

"Well, David," Mr. Levine says, extending his hand, "you've become quite an Internet sensation. You and Hammy."

My hand's sweaty, but I shake anyway. "Um, thank you."

Lindsay comes over and shoves her shoulder into mine.

Bubbe grins like crazy.

I take a deep breath.

Dad pats me on the back and nods.

"Obviously, your family's very proud," Mr. Levine says.

I think that Mom isn't here and she would like this, but then I look at Dad—he's beaming—and Bubbe and Lindsay, and I feel really good, even without Mom. But then I notice her tuba in the corner, and a little wave of sadness washes over me. It still feels like part of my family is missing.

"I'd like to ask you a few questions," Mr. Levine says. "And a photographer will be here to take some pictures."

"Okay," I say, but my voice cracks, and I'm glad this isn't a TV interview.

Mr. Levine asks if it's okay to tape-record our conversation.

I nod.

"You'll have to say it out loud for the tape recorder."

"Um, yes." I'm trembling. I can't believe Sophie kissed me. And Tommy and his friend tried to kill me. And now this.

With the tape recorder between us and its green light glowing, Mr. Levine asks me lots of questions, like "Are you a big fan of *The Daily Show?*" and "What's your favorite subject at school?" He grins after he asks this, and says, "And you can't cheat and say lunch."

No worries there. I wipe sweat off my upper lip and tell him that I'm a huge fan of *The Daily Show* and science is my favorite class.

When the photographer arrives, she takes pictures of me at my computer, me in front of fake New York, me holding Hammy and Hammy running on his wheel.

"Who gave you the hamster?" Mr. Levine asks.

I look down. "My mom."

I'm glad he doesn't ask any more questions.

After Mr. Levine and the photographer leave, Lindsay hits me in the back of the head. "David."

"Yeah?" I say, feeling the tiny hairs on the back of my neck stand up.

"You're like really, really famous."

"I guess," I say. *And when this article comes out, more people will be watching the Daily Acne Forecast. I'm sorry, Linds.*

Dad touches Lindsay's arm. "You okay with this?" Lindsay nods and tousles my hair.

Bubbe hugs me so tightly I suffocate for a little while. She puts my cheeks between her warm palms. "*Bubelah!* The *Philadelphia Inquirer.* Wait till Aunt Sherry hears about this!"

Dad leans over and whispers, "You know, David, your mom would be so proud."

I take a deep, shaky breath. "Yeah, maybe she'll . . ." But I don't finish the sentence.

51

In the morning, at the kitchen table, Bubbe hands me a toasted bagel. "So, how's our superstar?"

"Okay, I guess." I take a small bite, but it goes down hard because I'm worried about what might happen at school today.

"Next thing you know," Bubbe says, "you'll be on CNN or MSNBC or maybe even Oprah!"

I laugh.

Bubbe shoves a piece of bagel into her mouth. "Could happen."

"Hey, Bub, look at this." I push my face into hers.

She wipes bagel crumbs off my cheek.

"No," I say. "Look." I move closer.

"*Vos?*" she asks, squinting.

I turn the light on over the table and point to the corners of my upper lip. "See?"

Bubbe gets her glasses. "What am I looking for, *bubelah?*"

"My mustache."

"Pfft!" Bubbe waves her hand. "You call *that* a mustache?" She shoves her upper lip into my face. "Now, *that's* a mustache."

It's true. Bubbe's mustache is way darker than mine.

My shoulders droop. Even though I was interviewed by a reporter from the *Philadelphia Inquirer* yesterday, this is not good for my self-esteem.

52

I don't see Tommy in the courtyard before school. And my language arts teacher gives me a pass so I can go to the media center during lunch. I take a reading test on a computer and spend the rest of the period skimming magazines and looking longingly at the door to WHMS news.

In science class, I can hardly look at Sophie. *Is she going to kiss me again?*

"Here," she says, stuffing a piece of paper into my hand. "Call me after school."

While two girls demonstrate their board game about Marie Curie, I unfold the paper. It's Sophie's phone number with ten stars surrounding it. *Ten!*

I realize that the only way I'll be able to call Sophie after school is if I make it home, so when the buzzer sounds, I tear out of class. I'm the first person in the courtyard. I get home so fast that I stop to get the mail on my way in.

An ad for zit-be-gone cream, the water bill and Bubbe's *Oprah* magazine. Nothing from Mom.

53

In my room, I'm tempted to go online and check my videos' stats, but instead I grab the phone and pull the piece of paper with Sophie's number from my pocket. I count the stars again—ten—then begin to dial.

I check my watch—4:15—and realize that Sophie might not be home from school yet. I hang up. I'll wait another five minutes, then call.

"What do you think she wants?" I ask Hammy. "Do you think she might want to go out?"

Hammy is lying on his side on top of the wood shavings.

"Hammy?"

He's not moving, which is strange, because he usually responds when I talk to him. I slide the lid off and blow on him. His fur moves, but he doesn't.

"Ham—" My voice catches.

I lift him out. His fur is soft, but his body is stiff. His tiny dark eyes stare blankly at me.

I take Hammy to Lindsay's room. I don't knock on the door, just push it open.

"David, I'm—"

Lindsay hops off her bed. "What is that?" She comes closer and grabs my wrist. "Oh, my—"

I start shaking but hold Hammy out in my palm.

"Don't move." Lindsay runs to her closet and dumps out a shoe box full of envelopes. "Here," she says, offering me the empty box.

I can't put Hammy in an empty box. He needs his wood shavings and water bottle.

Lindsay shakes my wrist until Hammy falls into the box with a soft thud.

I still feel the weight of him on my palm.

Lindsay places the box on her bed and comes over to hug me. "Oh, David, I'm sorry. I know you loved that—"

But I'm gone. Down the steps and out of the house. I run faster than I've ever run in my life. I end up at Elliott's apartment building and pound on his door. A neighbor from across the hall peeks out, and I bolt. Away from Elliott. Away from home. Away from everything.

Run. Run. Run. But I can't outrun one thought: *Hammy's dead. The last thing Mom ever gave me is gone.*

54

It's dark by the time I get home, and the moon is out.

"Davey!" Bubbe shrieks. "*Oy vey*, I'm so glad you're home." She envelops me in a hug.

I cry, because I don't want *her* hugging me.

I want Hammy.

I want Mom.

When Bubbe finally lets me up for air, Dad puts a strong hand on my shoulder. "Lindsay told us. We're so sorry."

Lindsay shrugs.

I wipe my nose with my sleeve. "The average lifespan of a hamster is 2.5 years. Hammy didn't even live that long," I say, feeling cheated.

"It's not your fault," Dad says. "You did a real good job taking care of him."

"Yeah," Lindsay says. "And you have that cool video with him, right? *Hammy Time*. And the other ones, too."

I sniff. *Hammy was the real star of* TalkTime. *How am I ever going to make another one without him?*

"You were a good boy with him," Bubbe says.

"We saved dinner for you," Dad says.

"Matzo ball soup," Bubbe says.

"And I didn't steal all the matzo balls this time," Lindsay says, which makes me laugh and cry at the same time.

I swipe at my eyes. "I'm not hungry."

But Bubbe makes me sit and eat one matzo ball. And everyone watches.

Afterward, we go to the backyard. Lindsay holds the flashlight. Dad digs a hole near the azalea bush. I put Lindsay's shoe box with Hammy into the hole. And Bubbe says the Kaddish, the Jewish prayer for the dead.

Amen.

55

Please pick up. Please answer.

I wish I could call Elliott, but I can't. I really wish I could call Mom. She gave me Hammy. She deserves to know he's gone.

The phone rings four times before Ms. Meyers says, "Hello?"

"I know it's late, but is Sophie there?"

"David—"

"Please tell her it's really important that she call me back." I hang up. *Please call back, Sophie. Please.*

I go online and watch the *Hammy Time* video Elliott and I made. That video always cracks me up, but today it makes me sad. *How can Hammy be gone?* I drape a towel over his cage so I won't have to look at it.

When the phone rings, I grab it and hear Lindsay say hello. Then I hear Sophie's voice. "Got it, Linds," I say.

"Okay, David."

"Hi, Sophie."

"Hey, David. I thought you were going to call after school."

I look at the towel on top of Hammy's cage, and my throat constricts. "I need to tell you something."

"What?"

I take a raggedy breath. "Hammy's gone."

"Gone?"

"He died."

"Hammy's . . . dead?"

"Yup."

"Oh, David. I'm sorry."

"Thanks."

"Coming, Mom!" Sophie yells. Then she whispers, "I've got to hang up, but I'm going to give you something special tomorrow morning to cheer you up."

I wipe my nose with my sleeve again. "What?"

"You'll see."

I hold the phone long after the click.

After turning the phone's ringer off and setting my alarm clock, I pull my blanket to my chin and stare out the window. Hammy's out there in the cold ground while I'm lying in a warm bed. *It isn't fair!*

I have a hard time falling asleep.

56

When my alarm buzzes, my head feels stuffed with cotton. My eyes ache. I open crusty eyelids, see Hammy's covered cage, turn off the alarm and fall back to sleep.

When I wake again, it's brighter, but my eyes are still sore from crying so much. And my calf muscles ache from running yesterday. I yank the blanket over my head. *I'm not going to school today. It's the least I can do for Hammy.*

Then I remember we have a test in Ms. Lovely's class. I can't miss a test, especially in her class.

I force myself up and avoid looking at Hammy's cage while I dress.

Before leaving, I check my face in the mirror. My eyelids are pink and puffy. I hope they're a normal color by the time I get to school.

Dad intercepts me at the front door and gives me a fierce hug. "Love you, David."

I don't say anything, but Dad's hug and his words make me feel sad and strong at the same time. I walk to school, trying unsuccessfully not to think about how Hammy felt on my palm yesterday.

In the courtyard, I see the heavy kid from the TV studio. He's wearing a T-shirt that says "Fat kids are harder to kidnap."

"Hey," he says.

"Hey," I say back.

"I saw that article about you in the *Courier Times* and I checked out your stuff."

I nod.

"You're good."

"Thanks."

"You wanted to join the news team, right?"

"Yeah," I say, realizing that even though it seemed important before, it doesn't now.

"You should ask Ms. Petroccia again. You're really good."

"I thought it's only for seventh and eighth graders."

He shrugs. "You should ask."

When the bell buzzes, I rush to Ms. Lovely's class because I don't want to run into Tommy in the hallway. At my desk, I force myself to look over the chapter review. I hear a throat clearing and "Lameberg!"

What little energy I have drains. Holding my pencil feels like a Herculean effort, so I let it drop to my desk.

Sophie bounces in, clutching a brown paper bag.

How can she be so happy when Hammy's gone?

"This is for you," she whispers, holding up the bag.

It almost makes me glad I came to school today.

Sophie reaches into the bag and pulls out a cupcake—vanilla with yellow icing.

"Thank you," I whisper.

Ms. Lovely is still at the back of the classroom, near the door.

Sophie nods. "I'm really sorry about Hammy. He was so—"

"Lookie! It's Lameberg's birthday!"

I whirl around. Tommy waves. "Happy birthday, Lameberg."

"It's not my birthday. My ham—"

"Quiet in front," Ms. Lovely croaks.

I'm glad she said that, because I almost told Tommy about Hammy. And he doesn't deserve to know.

Ms. Lovely walks to the front of the room. "No food in my classroom, Mr. Greenberg."

Sophie snatches the cupcake off my desk and shoves it back into the bag.

Ms. Lovely smiles at her.

"Happy birthday, Lameberg!" Tommy calls again.

"It's not my birthday," I mutter through gritted teeth.

"Yeah, happy birthday!" another guy says.

"Happy birthday," a girl says.

Ms. Lovely levels the class with a stare. "You may celebrate Mr. Greenberg's birthday another time. Right now, we have a test."

It's not my birthday!

"Everything off your desks except your pencils."

The moment Ms. Lovely turns to grab the tests, I feel something bonk me on the back of the head.

I whirl around and glare at Tommy.

"Read it," he mouths, pointing to the wad of paper on the floor.

I take a deep breath and don't move.

"Read it," he says again, his voice menacing.

I try to resist, but snatch it, turn front and read.

Happy barfday, Lameberg. Will celubrate L8R.

As I shove the note into my backpack, my hand shakes. I can barely scrawl my name on the test that has landed on my desk, because now I realize exactly how Tommy Murphy plans to get me.

IT'S NOT MY BIRTHDAY!

57

By the time I get to science—the last class of the day—I've managed to avoid both Tommy Murphy and bathrooms, but I'm panicked.

I walk into class and take a deep, shaky breath, hoping I can hold it together.

Mr. Milot walks to the back of the room and grabs two metal trays. "Okay, class," he says, "today is Worm Dissection Day."

I'd forgotten about Worm Dissection Day.

A tray lands on our lab table, with a worm stretched out, held taut by pins.

I don't know if it's caused by the formaldehyde smell coming from the tray or seeing the dead worm with pins stuck in it, but a feeling swells inside my chest, and my throat squeezes.

"You okay?" Sophie asks, her fingers landing like a feather on my wrist.

It's hard not to cry when someone is being nice. A strangled sound comes from my throat, and my shoulders bob. I know that Niagara Falls is about to spill.

Mr. Milot, at the rear of the room, grabs two more trays, his back to the class.

Without asking, without a hall pass, without my backpack, I bolt.

I'm halfway down the hall when sadness overwhelms me. I lean back against a row of lockers and sink to the floor. My shoulders jerk and hot tears stream down my cheeks. I pull my knees to my chest and cover my face.

That's when I hear a door open at the far end of the hallway.

I squint and see the bald head of Mr. Carp.

I cover my own head with my arms. *Go away!* I peek through my arms and see Mr. Carp getting closer.

The door to the stairway is down the hall, past him. But the bathroom is right next to me.

"David?"

It's Mr. Milot, calling from science class.

"David Greenberg?"

I duck into the boys' bathroom, lean against the cool tile wall and hold my breath. *As soon as Mr. Carp passes, I'll run down the hall, away from science class, to the stairway and all the way home.*

A stall door opens and a cloud of cigarette smoke drifts out.

I hear a deep voice.

My jumbled thoughts distill to one: *Run!*

58

Too late.

Tommy Murphy saunters toward me, grinning.

"Lookie here," he says, poking me hard in the chest. "It's Lameberg. He thinks he's so cool with those dumb videos. Anybody could make them." He pokes me again. "You're not so special, Lameberg."

I shiver.

A big guy I don't recognize emerges from the same stall and stands beside Tommy. This kid has stubble on his chin. I think of the skimpy mustache hairs I showed Bubbe.

Cigarette smoke drifting from the stall reminds me of that summer day with Jack—the day he warned me to avoid the bathroom on the second floor near the science wing.

"Hey," Tommy says, shoving the other guy. "We don't need to get him after school today. Lameberg came to us. Can you believe it?" Tommy gets in my face. "Mighty nice of you, Lameberg."

I close my eyes and pray.

Let it be quick.

And painless.

His warm tobacco breath on my face, Tommy says, "It's time to celebrate your birthday, Lameberg."

"Yeah," the other guy says. "Happy birthday."

Tommy's so close to my face, I see rubber bands stretching between his braces. I feel cold, hard wall pressed against my back.

And I hear something. Mr. Carp whistling softly. Tommy's eyes open wide. *Scream, David. Scream!* I don't even breathe as I hear Mr. Carp's whistling get softer and softer and then . . . nothing.

Tommy presses his lips together, and there are hands on my arms and shoulders. They drag me to the stall door.

When Tommy kicks open the door, I twist like crazy. "Mr. Carp!" I yell, but a damp hand clamps over my mouth. It smells like cigarette smoke.

I jerk hard and scream a muffled "No!"

Someone leans close to my ear. "The only thing I wanna hear out of you, Lameberg, is 'Happy Birthday.' " He twists my arm behind my back for emphasis.

I shake my head and struggle wildly, but they've got me in an iron grip. "Sing!" Tommy says.

I shake my head again, afraid to open my mouth.

Then his words get deep and ominous. "Sing or we'll drown you."

I look at the toilet. There's nothing in it except water . . . and germs and bacteria. If there are 516,000 bacteria in one square inch of armpit, I don't want to think about how many are swarming inside that toilet bowl. Tears stream down my cheeks. "Happy birthday to me," I cry, even though it's nowhere near my stupid birthday. "Happy birth—"

"What's going on in here?"

Thank God! My arms go limp.

Tommy and his friend drag me out of the stall.

It's the big guy who wears funny T-shirts. When he sees me, his eyes open wide. "Hold on, kid. I'll get help."

And he runs out of the bathroom.

Don't go!

"Uh, Tommy," the other guy says, "I gotta go. If I get in trouble again, my dad'll kill me." He lets go of my arm and leaves.

"Wuss!" Tommy yells after him, squeezing my arms with visegrip hands. He looks toward the stall and grunts. "Let's get this done."

"No!" I scream. "Get off me!"

Even though I flail and kick, Tommy forces me back into the stall, his hands on my upper arms, his body pressed against my back until I'm facing the toilet.

"No!"

"Got to," Tommy says, squeezing my arms so hard it feels like his fingers are boring holes through my bones. "I owe you."

In one swift motion, Tommy grabs the back of my neck and shoves my head into the water.

Then flushes.

59

My forehead splashes into the toilet bowl and bumps porcelain. Water rushes loudly around my ears.

I force my head backward and am suddenly standing tall, rivulets dripping into my ears and down my neck.

I'm alone, heaving and blubbering, but won't open my mouth. *Can't let that water get into my mouth.*

Shivering, I splash water from the sink onto my face and neck. There are no paper towels, so I walk out of the bathroom dripping.

I hear a gasp and turn.

"David?" Mr. Milot says.

I'm staring at my science teacher and my entire class standing behind him. Sophie's hand is clamped over her mouth.

The big guy shakes his head. "Sorry, kid. I tried—"

But I don't hear another word. My vision blurs. And I take off, my sneakers squeaking down the hallway.

A boy twirling a hall pass turns to look at me.

I run down the stairs and toward the main doors.

"Hey!" a deep voice calls. "Stop!"

I keep running.

Past the doors into the blaring sunshine, beyond the car line. *They see me. They all see me dripping. I guess I'm not that funny kid in the videos now. I'm not an Internet phenom or a celeb in the newspaper. I'm just wet, humiliated Lameberg.*

I trip on a crack in the sidewalk and windmill my arms. I feel like I did when I knew I was going to fall into the pool this summer. But I don't fall. I run.

Past the crossing guard.

Past a lady walking her dog.

Past houses and bushes and mailboxes.

I run until I'm home, out of breath and fumbling with my key. Dad's car is gone. Bubbe's car is gone, too.

Inside, it's quiet. Everything looks the same but feels different.

I charge upstairs. To the bathroom.

And once I'm locked inside, I sink to the tile floor.

And weep.

Middle

School

SUCKS!!!

60

I'm in my room with the door locked, lying flat on my bed.

"Go away!" I yell.

"But, *bubelah*, I made peach kugel. Your favorite."

"I hate that. Go away."

"Davey, I'm sorry about Hammy, but you have to eat something. A little *nashn*?"

"No!" *I won't go downstairs. Or back to school. How can I face those kids from science class? They saw me dripping! Tommy humiliated me and he'll probably do it again . . . and again. Elliott still hates me, and I don't even know why. What good does it do to have thousands of fans online when not a single person at school likes me except Sophie? I can still see her hand slapped over her mouth as she watched me dripping toilet water onto the floor. How am I supposed to deal with all of this without Hammy to make me feel better? Without Mom?*

A little while after Bubbe leaves, someone pounds on my

bedroom door. "David Todd Greenberg, open up this second. You've upset your bubbe."

"Sorry," I say, even though I'm not.

"Open. The. Door," Dad says.

I say nothing.

He pounds once. Hard. "Now."

I look at the towel over Hammy's cage, pull my covers up to my nose and say nothing.

"Well, then . . ." Dad sounds exasperated. "You won't eat dinner tonight."

"Fine," I say, because that was all I wanted in the first place.

An hour later, another knock.

"David, Sophie's on the phone."

She probably wants to tell me she never wants to see me again. My heart beats so loudly in my ears I think I'm going to go deaf.

"Hello?" Lindsay says, sounding annoyed. "She wants to know what you want her to do with your cupcake. Whatever the heck that means."

The cupcake. The cupcake that started this whole thing. Tommy wouldn't have even thought of flushing my head if he hadn't seen the cupcake and figured it was my birthday.

"Tell her I don't care. Tell her she can flush it down the toilet!" I don't mean that. I know that Sophie was just trying to make me feel better about Hammy with that cupcake, but I'm too upset right now to be nice. Besides, I can't stand knowing that she saw me dripping.

"I'm not saying that," Lindsay hisses.

"Go away!" I scream, and throw my Rubik's Cube at the door.

I thought I'd be glad when the hallway light finally went out and I heard Dad shut his bedroom door, but I'm not. Even though I could turn on my computer right now and read dozens of fan messages from people all over the world, I feel more alone than ever.

61

"School," Dad says, pounding on my door in the morning.

"Ugh," I groan.

"Are you sick, David? Let me in."

"Not sick," I say. "Not going."

"Son." Dad's voice softens. "You have to go."

"Not going."

He slams his hand on the door; then I hear footsteps fade. *Not going to school. Not dealing with Tommy Murphy and his lunch table full of Neanderthals or Elliott or even Sophie. Not going to hear "Lameberg" ever again.*

Just not.

At ten-forty-five, I use the bathroom, brush my teeth and catch my image in the mirror. I look worn out, like Dad looks sometimes. And my eyes are still pink and puffy.

I sneak down to the kitchen and bring up supplies—orange juice, a sliced bagel, three pieces of cheese and a cereal bar.

Then I lock my door again.

I turn on the computer and am surprised that I'm able to smile about the huge number of new views and comments the videos have gotten. *How can one part of my life be so amazing while the other part, well . . . is flushed down the toilet? If only a few of these fans went to Harman, my life would be so much better.*

I don't answer the phone when it rings twice in the late afternoon. Sophie leaves a message. "David, I want to know if you're okay. I'll drop your backpack off in front of your house later. Call me. And let me know if you want the math homework."

Nope.

The other message is from Elliott. *Elliott!* "David, look, Tommy told me what happened and I'm . . . I'm really . . ." He chokes up. "Look, I'm really sorry, okay?"

I take a deep breath and play the message again. *Nope. Definitely not okay!*

I don't answer my family when they pound on my bedroom door in the evening—until Dad threatens to take the door off its hinges. I'm not sure if he can do it, because he's pretty hopeless with tools, but I open the door a crack just in case.

"I'm okay," I tell him, even though I'm not. "But I'm not coming out."

"Yes, you are," Dad says, bounding into my room. "And you're going to school tomorrow."

I cross my arms. "No, I'm not."

"You are," Dad says.

"I'm not, because tomorrow is Saturday."

Dad's neck gets red. "Well, Monday. You're definitely going back Monday."

"Never going back."

"You are," Dad says, sitting on my bed and patting the space beside him. "Now, let's talk about this."

"No." I know I sound like a baby, but I don't care. And I don't sit beside him, either.

"You'll feel better, David. I promise if you talk about this, you'll feel better."

"Talking will not make me feel better," I say, crossing my arms more tightly. *Tommy getting transferred to another school would make me feel better. Tommy getting suspended for life would make me feel better. Tommy getting arrested and sent to jail until I graduate from college would make me feel fantastic.*

"David, I love you."

My anger dissipates.

Dad sighs. "Well, good night." He stands and kisses the top of my head. "I'll be in my room." He takes a few steps toward my door. "If you want to talk."

"I don't."

Dad leaves, and no one else comes in.

After a while, I go to the living room and sit on the couch in the dark near Mom's tuba. I turn away from it and remember the time Mom and I camped in the living room. She wasn't up for camping outside, so we moved the coffee table, pitched a tent she had ordered online, popped Paul Newman's popcorn and drank grape juice from a canteen. Then we watched *The Daily Show* through the tent flap late into the night.

I also remember that first day of summer break, when Elliott and I were supposed to watch the *Daily Show* episodes I'd recorded, but ended up going to the stupid mall.

I turn on the TV and click on the first of many *Daily Show* episodes I recorded. During Jon's opening monologue, I don't laugh, even though he's funny. I love the expressions he makes, especially when he raises one eyebrow and says, "Oh, really?" Elliott used to do that when we made *TalkTime* together. I can't believe he called today. Maybe he's changing into a decent person. Maybe he wants to be friends again. Or maybe it's just another trick. Doesn't matter. It's too late. The damage has already been done.

By the second episode of *The Daily Show*, I laugh a couple of times. It feels good to laugh.

"Hey."

It's Lindsay, wearing her Dumb Bunny pajamas. She sits at the other end of the couch. "Mind if I watch?"

I shrug, but I'm glad she's here. And even more glad when she laughs at Jon's jokes, too. "He's freakin' hilarious," she says, and for some reason it feels like she's saying it about me.

Bubbe walks in with three bowls of caramel swirl ice cream, one for each of us. She plops onto the couch between me and Lindsay. "This guy's a real mensch," she says between spoonfuls.

Dad comes in, too, and sits in the chair. I catch him looking at me and nodding.

Together, we watch two more shows before Dad says, "I've got to turn in. I'm exhausted."

"Me too," Bubbe says, and kisses my forehead.

Lindsay slides next to me and bumps my shoulder with hers. "Night, David."

"Night," I say, feeling better than I have in a long time, which is crazy, because my hamster is dead and I had my head flushed. *And it wasn't even my birthday*. But watching Jon Stewart reminds me of what I want to do when I grow up, of what I'm really good at doing right now.

Upstairs, even though I'm so tired I'm dizzy, I take Hammy's cage and dump out the wood shavings. I scrub the bottom, too. Then I carry the cage, water bottle and food dish to the garage.

It hurts too much to keep looking at that empty cage.

"Good-bye, Hammy."

62

Saturday morning, I wake to Bubbe's shrieking.

I trip getting out of bed and run downstairs, figuring I'll see a shiny black water bug skitter near her feet. She hates those things.

Instead, I see Dad and Lindsay at the kitchen table with Bubbe, fussing over the newspaper.

Lindsay grabs it and reads the headline. " 'Local Boy and His Hamster Become Internet Phenomenon.' "

"Davey, you're famous!" Bubbe squeezes my cheeks in her palms and kisses me hard on the forehead. "My grandson the phenomenon. The *Philadelphia Inquirer*! I hope your aunt Sherry is reading this."

I picture Cousin Jack giving me extra noogies next time he sees me.

Dad grabs the newspaper and reads.

"Out loud," Lindsay says.

Dad reads about how I started making *TalkTime* and how

Jon Stewart is my idol. There's a photo of me and Hammy, which makes me totally choke up. I think of his empty cage in the garage and how much he'd have loved to pee on this article.

"David, this is amazing," Dad says, tapping the article. "We're going to have to go out and buy lots of—"

The phone rings.

"It's the reporter from the *Courier Times*," Lindsay says. "He wants to do a follow-up article on you."

After I answer his questions and hang up, the phone rings again. It's Dad's friend Alan Drummond. "Hey, David. Saw the article about you when I was at the gym this morning. Congratulations, man!"

I blush. "Thanks."

Alan Wexler calls, too, and congratulates me.

So does Jack. "Way to go, little man. It's cool having a famous cousin. Does Lindsay know about the—"

"Yeah," I say, feeling bad all over again, because now more people will see Lindsay's cream-covered face in the Daily Acne Forecast. I wish I'd never put that in the videos.

Three people request radio interviews. Two newspaper reporters, four neighbors and, it seems, most of Bensalem and approximately half of the rest of the country call. Even Ms. Meyers, Mr. Carp and Ms. Petroccia call to congratulate me.

I can't believe it. I'm so busy answering the phone, I don't have time to go online, but I imagine there are a lot more messages than usual and even more views and comments for my videos.

At eleven o'clock, when I'm in bed and the phone has finally stopped ringing, I realize that one person hasn't called—one person who probably hasn't seen the article but couldn't call even if she had.

Mom.

I shuffle into the hallway and see light shining under Lindsay's door. I knock.

"Yeah?"

Lindsay's in bed, reading *Ella Minnow Pea*. She puts the book down.

"Hey," I say.

"Hey, David. What's up?" She pats the edge of her bed.

I sit and tell her all about Tommy Murphy and how he gave me a swirlie.

Lindsay's quiet for a while, then says, "Tommy Murphy's a jerk. It wasn't even your birthday." She opens her arms. I fall into them, and Lindsay gives me a bone-crunching hug.

63

Sunday, in Hebrew school, the cantor tells me he read about me in the newspaper. "Very impressive, David," he says. A few kids tell me how much they like my videos. I wish the kids from Hebrew school went to Harman.

As soon as I get home, I put up fake New York. I know I have to make another *TalkTime*. My fans are waiting.

When I get to the Top Six and a Half list, I say, "Top Six and a Half Ways to Avoid a Swirlie." And something happens that has never happened before. My mind goes blank. I can't think of a single way to avoid a swirlie. I don't even know what I did to make Tommy Murphy hate me so much.

I put my camera away and stare out the window at the place in the backyard near the azalea bush.

What good does it do to be famous online when in real life, I go to a school where all I am is "Lameberg"?

64

The next morning, I button my collared shirt and plod downstairs, a knot squeezing tight in my stomach because I don't want to go back to school.

In the kitchen, Bubbe pats the chair beside her. "I have five minutes before I leave. Sit."

I sit and let out a sigh.

"Frosted flakes or shredded wheat?"

"Shredded."

Bubbe puts the bowl in front of me and lays her warm hand on mine. "Middle school can be hard." She looks in my eyes. "Harder for some than others. Lindsay told me what happened."

"Oh, great." I shove a spoonful of shredded wheat into my mouth. "No offense, Bubbe," I say with my mouth full, "but you don't understand."

"I understand more than you think, David."

I nod but know she doesn't. No one does, except maybe that

boy Lindsay told me about who got a swirlie and ended up trans-ferring schools.

"Now that you're famous, things should go better in school, no?"

No.

Bubbe taps her watch. "I've got to go." She kisses my forehead and says, "You'll do fine today, Davey."

"Thanks," I say, and dump the rest of my cereal into the sink. *How will I possibly do fine when so many people saw me dripping toilet water and Tommy Murphy might still want to kill me?*

In the courtyard, kids hang around in groups. They talk and laugh and shove each other. Even though I feel like I have a neon sign on my forehead that says Lameberg Got a Swirlie, no one seems to notice me.

Sophie runs over and gives me a hug.

I'm shocked that she doesn't seem even a little repulsed by the germs that were on me from the swirlie.

Sophie hands me a brown paper bag. "It's stale, but . . ."

The cupcake.

"Thanks," I say, and look around for people making fun of me. No one seems to be.

When the bell buzzes, I walk slowly, like I'm heading to the gallows. That's kind of what facing math class with Ms. Lovely and Tommy Murphy feels like sometimes.

"Hurry up," Sophie says, yanking on my sleeve.

As always, Ms. Lovely stands at the classroom door. She's smiling. At least, I think it's a smile. Hard to tell through all those wrinkles. "Welcome back, Mr. Greenberg."

When I'm seated, I turn and look at Tommy Murphy. He's

glaring at me like he's pissed. *What does he have to be mad about? I'm the one who should be mad!*

Ms. Lovely leans over and quietly says, "I read the *Inquirer* article this weekend." And she winks at me.

I sink low in my seat.

Ms. Lovely turns on the TV, and we stand for the pledge. I'm not paying attention to what Ellen Winser says, because I'm trying to figure out why Tommy could possibly still be mad.

That's when I hear my name.

Ellen Winser is talking about *me* on TV. She says, "Our very own David Greenberg, a sixth grader here at Harman, was mentioned in the *Philadelphia Inquirer* this weekend."

A gasp spreads around the room. Ms. Lovely beams.

I forgot that when Ms. Petroccia called my house, she asked if it would be okay to mention the article on WHMS news today.

Ellen talks about the article, then shows the *Hammy Time* video.

I get choked up watching Hammy, but kids laugh. And when it's over, the class applauds. I can even hear applause from other classrooms, and it feels amazing.

Ellen Winser says, "When you see David in the hallway, congratulate him." And they flash a picture of me in front of fake New York.

My neck gets hot.

"And in other news . . ."

Kids do stop me in the hallway as I walk to my next class. People I don't know slap me on the back and say, "Funny video, man." Gavin gives me a thumbs-up in the lunchroom, and a couple of guys from his table hoot and whistle when I walk past.

I feel pretty good as I move toward the back.

"Hey, Lameberg!" Tommy screams, and the guys at his table crack up. "Think you're hot stuff, huh?"

Why can't you leave me alone? I bow my head, but before I do, I notice that Elliott isn't sitting at the Neanderthals' table. I look around the lunchroom but don't see him.

When I put my tray down, a couple of the kids nod, and the girl stops reading long enough to smile and say, "Funny video this morning."

"Thanks," I say, biting into my grilled cheese sandwich, but inside my head, I keep hearing *Hey, Lameberg! Hey, Lameberg!*

"Hey."

I stop chewing and whirl around, expecting to see Tommy Murphy and the Neanderthals, which I realize sounds like a name for a band. I should probably suggest it to Dad.

Standing behind me is Elliott. He's holding a tray and wearing the now stained shirt he wore on the first day of school. His eyebrows arch, like he's waiting for me to say something.

"Mind?" he asks, nodding toward the seat beside me.

I shrug, and he puts his tray on the table and sits next to me.

At first I wonder if it's another trick, but it doesn't feel like a trick. And when Tommy yells, "Hey, Lameberg and friend of Lameberg," and Elliott gives Tommy the finger, I know it's not a trick. I know that Elliott has finally crossed back over from the dark side.

"Wow," I say.

Elliott shrugs. "He's a jerk."

"I know," I say. "But—"

"I was a bigger jerk for hanging out with him."

"Yeah, but—"

"Look, don't worry about it." Elliott rips a ketchup packet open with his teeth. "You gonna eat those fries?"

I throw a few fries onto Elliott's tray, and it feels like the most natural thing in the world.

He and I eat grilled cheese and fries and nudge each other's shoulders every once in a while. We don't say anything else, but it's the best lunch I've had since coming to Harman.

When the bell buzzes, I realize that Dad was right. He said that I just had to give it time, that things would work out with Elliott. And it looks like they are working out.

Maybe this means things might work out with Mom, too.

65

When I walk into science class, everyone stares. I think it's because of the announcement on the news this morning, but then I remember. The last time these people saw me, my head was dripping as I came out of the bathroom.

"You okay, David?" Mr. Milot asks, his hand on my shoulder.

Someone bursts out laughing.

Mr. Milot stares at her, and she mutters, "Sorry."

I'm relieved when Mr. Milot starts talking about the properties of protons. I'm really relieved when the bell buzzes and my first post-swirlie school day ends the same way it began, with Sophie hugging me.

66

After school, I walk Sophie to her mom's car.

"Want a ride home?" she asks.

"Nah," I say. "I'm waiting for someone."

" 'Kay. See you tomorrow," Sophie says.

I watch their car drive away with Sophie waving to me out the back window. I turn around and realize I'm standing in the courtyard—alone—a giant bull's-eye for Tommy Murphy.

Elliott walks over. "Hey, David."

"Hey," I say.

"You want to—"

Tommy Murphy charges toward Elliott and slams into him so hard he goes flying. Elliott is sprawled on the ground, his backpack a couple of feet ahead of him.

Kids turn and stare.

Tommy stands with his chest pushed forward. "Why you talking to Lameberg?" He motions to me. "Now that he's famous and all, you dump me, right? I ain't good enough for ya?"

Elliott stands, brushes off his pants and faces Tommy. "You're a jerk." Elliott bends to pick up his backpack, but Tommy shoves him again.

Then he comes over to me.

My legs go weak. Tommy stands so close I smell cigarette smoke on his breath.

He pokes me hard in the chest. "Lameberg!"

Elliott takes a running start and slams into Tommy so hard Tommy stumbles sideways. "Don't call him that! Don't talk to him! Don't even look at him!"

Tommy breathes hard through his nose and tilts his head, like a bull preparing to charge. "Oh, mama has to protect her little baby. I'll call Lameberg whatever I want to call him, friend of Lameberg."

Elliott looks around at the kids forming a circle and smiles. "Then I'll tell everyone that you—"

Tommy slams into Elliott again. "I'll kill you if you—"

"What's going on here?" Mr. Carp says through his megaphone. "Break this up."

Tommy steps back. "Uh, nothing, Mr. Carp. We're just . . . we're cool."

Mr. Carp looks at Elliott for confirmation.

Elliott looks at Tommy. "Yeah, nothing's going on. We're cool, right?"

Tommy nods. "Yeah, right."

Mr. Carp says, "Mr. Murphy, don't you have enough detentions already? Move along."

Tommy lets out a big breath and jogs off.

"You all right, Mr. Greenberg?" Mr. Carp asks, even though I'm not the one who got shoved.

"Yeah, I guess so," I say, looking at Elliott.

"Great article in the paper," he says. "I knew you'd turn it around."

As soon as Mr. Carp walks away, I say to Elliott, "Thanks."

He tilts his head. "No problem."

As we walk home, I say, "What do you call a Neanderthal with only half a brain?"

"What?" Elliott asks, chucking a pinecone at a stop sign.

"Someone twice as smart as Tommy Murphy."

Elliott shakes his head, then bumps his shoulder into mine. I can tell he's as happy to be walking home together as I am.

"So, what dirt do you have on Tommy?" I ask.

"When we were friends or whatever, we used to just walk into each other's apartments. Our folks were never home, you know."

I nod. Elliott's mom works all the time, but Elliott isn't supposed to have friends in the apartment when she's not there.

"Anyway," Elliott says, "one time I walked in, and Tommy was sitting there watching that little kids' show *Dora the Explorer*."

I remember Tommy's face an inch from mine when he had me cornered in the bathroom. "*Dora the Explorer*? Really?"

"Yup," Elliott says. "He made some lame excuse that he was just switching channels, but he wasn't. I stood back awhile before he knew I was there, and he was actually watching it. And laughing."

"Oh my gosh. Does he have a little brother or sister or something?"

"Nope," Elliott says. "Just him."

We both crack up.

"Hey," I say. "Maybe we could use that in our next *TalkTime*."

"I miss making them, but I'm going to save that little bit of dirt for an emergency. I think it's good for both of us to have something hanging over Tommy Murphy's head."

"Definitely."

When we get to my house, I feel awkward because Elliott hasn't been over in such a long time. I'm afraid if I invite him in, he'll make some lame excuse, but things have been going so well that I ask anyway. "Want to come in for a while?"

Elliott lets out a big breath. "Heck, yeah. I don't want to go home and find that Neanderthal waiting for me."

"Oh, right. I didn't think of that."

I grab the mail and head for the front door. Peeking from the envelopes is a letter with *XOXO* over the return address. It's for me. From Mom. I push the letter back into the stack. I'll read it later, after Elliott leaves.

67

Lindsay's in the living room, doing homework on the couch. She looks up and there's surprise in her eyes. "Elliott," she says. "Haven't seen you in a while."

He nods, his cheeks reddening.

The phone rings, and Lindsay grabs it.

"Wanna hang out in my room?" I ask Elliott.

"Okay."

"I'm Ms. Greenberg," Lindsay says, winking at us.

I nudge Elliott and nod toward the phone. "Check this out," I whisper. "Lindsay's so funny with telemarketers."

Elliott and I hunch together and eavesdrop.

"Yes, he's my son," Lindsay says, shrugging at me and Elliott.

It's hard to hold back laughter.

"Yes," Lindsay says, "that would be wonderful. I'll let him know."

She presses the phone against her ear and leans forward.

"No, thank *you*. He'll be very excited to hear that."

She nods.

"Yes, just let me get some paper." Lindsay waves her hand, and Elliott whips a sheet of paper and a pen from his backpack.

Lindsay scribbles something, then says, "Thanks again. Good-bye."

When Lindsay hangs up, her cheeks are bright pink and her hands are flapping. She looks at me, then Elliott, then me again. "David," she says in this high-pitched voice that sends my heart racing.

"What?"

Lindsay screams, "They're showing *TalkTime* on *The Daily Show*!"

I hear something that sounds like *"TalkTime"* and *"The Daily Show."*

I shake my head. "What?"

She keeps flapping her hands, like she's hoping to take flight. "David, they're going to put *TalkTime* on *The Daily Show*."

"They're . . ."

"On tomorrow's show!"

Elliott punches me really hard in the arm. "David, this is so great. This is so great."

Lindsay holds both of my hands. "That was a producer from *The Daily Show*. They're going to play your Jon Stewart *TalkTime* video."

"Oh, my . . ."

Lindsay squeezes my hands really hard and we jump and scream. Elliott pumps his fists in the air. "Oh, yeah! Sweet! Oh, yeah!"

Dad walks in just as Lindsay and I fall over and nearly crack our heads on the coffee table.

"What? What are we celebrating?" Dad asks. "Hey, Elliott. Great to see you." He squeezes Elliott's shoulder. "So, what's going on here?"

Breathless, Lindsay explains. "A producer . . . from *The Daily Show* called. They found out . . . about David's videos . . . on their forum. And they're playing his video . . . tomorrow."

"*The Daily Show?*" Dad asks. "Are you sure it wasn't somebody playing a trick?"

Lindsay shows Dad the piece of paper.

Dad calls the number and speaks to the producer. He hangs up and says, "It's true."

Lindsay and I jump and scream all over again.

"*Vos?*" Bubbe asks, coming into the room.

Lindsay explains, and Bubbe hugs me. "Oh, I'm so proud. I told you that Jon Stewart was a mensch!" Then she notices Elliott.

"*Bubelah!*" She puts his cheeks in her palms. "So nice to have you back here." Bubbe looks at me and winks.

"Nice to see you, too, Matzo Ball Mama," Elliott says, and we all crack up.

68

"We should have a party," Lindsay says.

Dad reels back. "A party?"

"Yeah. Let's have a bunch of people over to watch *The Daily Show* together."

"I don't know," Dad says. "It's a school night."

Lindsay puts a hand on her hip and gives Dad "the look."

"Okay," he says. "I get it. This is a really big deal."

"Yeah," she shrieks. "My little brother's video is going to be on *The Daily Show*." She messes up my hair.

I duck out of the way and say, "Quit it," but inside it feels really good.

Dad scratches his chin. "I guess we could invite Alan Drummond and Alan Wexler."

"And Sherry and the kids," Bubbe says.

"And a couple of my friends," Lindsay chimes in.

"And Sophie," I say.

Elliott elbows me in the ribs.

"And her mom," Dad says.

"And Tommy Murphy," Elliott says.

Lindsay grabs a pillow from the couch and chucks it at him.

"Kidding. I was kidding." He puts his arms up in self-defense.

It feels so good to have Elliott back.

Dad scans the living room. "I guess if we move the coffee table out and add some chairs and—"

"I'll make appetizers," Bubbe says.

"I'll make seven-layer dip," Lindsay says.

"And we should have popcorn," I say, thinking of the night Mom and I camped out and watched *The Daily Show* together.

"Popcorn's good," Bubbe says. "And punch. I'll make a big bowl of fruit punch."

Dad looks around again, like he's imagining the room full of people. His gaze stops at the tuba. He walks to the corner and picks it up with a grunt. "I guess it's time we got rid of this thing."

My heart squeezes. I remember that awful night with mom and dad and the tuba.

Lindsay sidles up beside Dad. "Definitely," she says. "Let's put it on Craigslist."

"Or eBay," Elliott says. "My cousin sold a pair of used shoes on eBay and got twenty bucks."

"Or in the garbage," Bubbe says, crossing her arms.

I take a deep breath. "I have a better idea."

Everyone looks at me.

69

Before I know it, we're piled in Dad's car, heading to Sophie's house, the tuba heavy on my lap. I'm squished in the backseat between Lindsay and Elliott.

When Ms. Meyers opens the door, she invites us in and yells upstairs, "Sophie, company. Come down."

That's when I notice something's missing—the Spanish name tags. The stairs are just stairs. The door is just a door. And I remember Sophie telling me her mom finally took the labels down and is loosening up.

Sophie comes downstairs, her curls bouncing.

"Hey," she says, tilting her head.

"Hey," I say, and hand her Mom's tuba.

Dad clears his throat. "We won't be needing this anymore, and we thought you might enjoy playing it."

Sophie squirrels air in her cheeks and lets out a blast.

We all laugh, and Ms. Meyers covers her ears.

"We'll get you some lessons, honey," she says, patting Sophie's shoulder. "The music school would probably give me a discount now."

Sophie puts the tuba down. "Mom's teaching trumpet a couple nights a week over at J.A.M.—Jupiter Academy of Music." She looks at her mom. "She read some advice in that newspaper column 'Alan's Answers' that made her think of it."

Dad coughs.

"So . . . ," Bubbe says.

"Thanks for the tuba, David." Sophie leans over and kisses my cheek.

I break out in pepperminty shivers.

On the way home, Elliott elbows me. "You are so lucky."

I put my hands behind my head. "Yeah."

And we both crack up.

When we get home, I show Elliott the mean video Tommy made when he tripped me in the lunchroom. "At least there aren't any comments," I say.

"Yeah," Elliott says, "but it's got thirty-five views."

"I know. That stinks," I say, but I don't tell Elliott that most of those are probably mine.

Elliott takes over my keyboard.

"What are you—"

He writes a comment on Tommy's video: *This video sux!—Dora*

We crack up and high-five.

70

The next morning, I ask Dad if I can stay home from school because my video will be on *The Daily Show*.

He says no, but I don't really mind, because Elliott and I are walking to school together.

Just before the intersection, Elliott asks, "What's the difference between a rock and Tommy Murphy?"

I shrug.

"A rock has more personality."

I shove my shoulder into Elliott's. "Good one."

Ms. Lovely hands me a note as soon as I walk into class.

"Ms. Petroccia, the media specialist, wants to see you," she says and hands me a hall pass.

Sophie looks at me and tilts her head.

I shrug.

Tommy Murphy scowls, but I ignore him and head to the media center.

Inside the TV studio, the heavy guy turns to me. His T-shirt reads "Fat. Not Pregnant." "Here he is," he says to Ms. Petroccia.

"David," she says, putting a hand on my shoulder, "we were wondering if you'd like to do a special segment on WHMS news. You know, something short and funny, kind of like your videos, but appropriate for Harman. Maybe once a week or so."

I stare at her. This is even better than I imagined—more fun than just being a newscaster. I can create funny skits about the teachers and the lunchroom. Maybe Elliott can even help.

"If you feel it's too much . . . I just thought, you know, since you do such a good job with your videos . . ."

"No," I say. "It would be awesome, but I thought only seventh graders—"

"In your case," Ms. Petroccia says, grinning, "I think we can make an exception."

The heavy kid high-fives me, then holds up his hand to signal Ellen Winser that it's time to start.

"Come here tomorrow during fifth period," Ms. Petroccia says. "I'll send your teacher a note. And we'll go over everything."

I feel great as I walk back to class. I can't wait to tell Elliott about this at lunch.

71

About a half hour before everyone's supposed to arrive for the party, I grab some popcorn from a bowl on the kitchen counter and notice Mom's letter on top of the mail. With all that happened yesterday, I forgot to read it.

I take the letter to my room, sit at my desk and look at the place where Hammy's cage used to be. I check online and see that *Hammy Time* has nearly two million views. And Magazine Cover Jon Stewart has over a million. I'm sure that after tonight, that number will spike even higher.

I switch off the computer, move to my bed and carefully open the envelope.

Dear David,
    Lindsay wrote to me and told me about Hammy.

"What?" I say out loud. "Not possible." I drop the letter onto my bed and knock on Lindsay's door.

"Enter if you're famous."

I smile and go in.

Lindsay's on her bed, polishing her fingernails. The smell stings my nose.

"Hey," I say, wiping my nose with the back of my hand.

"Hey yourself. Ready for tonight?"

I shrug. "Lindsay, can I ask you one question?"

"Shoot."

"You said you'd never write to Mom, right?"

"Right. That was one question. You're done."

"Ha-ha." I sit on the end of her bed.

"Watch it," she says, wiping polish off her fingertip.

"Sorry, Linds. Did you write to Mom? About me?"

She stops polishing and looks at me. "You were really upset after Hammy died. I didn't know what else to do." She shrugs. "Lot of good it did. It's not like Mom called or visited or anything."

"She wrote me a letter," I say. I walk over and kiss my sister on the cheek, which is practically zit free. "Thank you."

"You're welcome, David. Now get out before you mess up my polish."

I smile and head back to my room to finish reading Mom's letter.

When Lindsay wrote me that letter, I decided I needed to visit you.

My heart races. I almost run back into Lindsay's room to tell her Mom's going to visit.

I tried, David. I tried a hundred different times, but I couldn't make myself leave the house and get into the car. Marcus tried to help, but I just couldn't do it.

I remember how Mom used to freak out if she thought she'd have to leave the house when she lived here. Sometimes she even got upset if someone called on the phone for her, and she'd refuse to answer it. Come to think of it, it was amazing Mom was able to leave at all to go live with the Farmer in Maine.

I'm sorry, David. I'm sorry about Hammy. You have no idea how much I wanted to drive to the pet place in the mall and surprise you with a new hamster. I imagined the scene a million times.

Me too. But the pet place in the mall is closed, anyway.

About once a month, I'm able to walk with Marcus to the public library. It's a long walk, but I do it so I can watch your videos, David. You've gotten so many comments lately, I hope you can still find mine—LADM—Lindsay and David's Mom.

"You're LADM?" I say out loud.

I'm sorry I couldn't be everything your dad needed me to be. I hope he's happy anyway. I'm sorry I couldn't be what Lindsay needed me to be, but I'm so glad she finally wrote to me. And I'm sorry I can't be there for you, David. Please keep me in your heart.
Love and candy corn,
Mom

I sniff hard and press Mom's letter to my chest. *She tried,* I think. *She really tried.*

The doorbell rings.

"Got it," Dad calls.

"Hey, where's the big star?" I hear Alan Drummond say downstairs.

I fold the letter and slip it back into the envelope. Then I tuck it into the shoe box in my closet with the other dozens of letters from Mom. "Love you," I say, and head downstairs.

72

"Hey," Alan Drummond says, raising his glass to me. "You're a real star, David."

"Thanks," I say, and duck my head.

The front door opens, and Aunt Sherry, Amy, Rachel and Jack walk in. Rachel pinches me. "Hi, David. Mom said I could stay up late to watch your show."

"That's great, Rach." I rub my arm where she pinched it.

Jack gets me in a killer headlock and gives me noogies. "How cool is this, Cuz?"

"Cool," I gasp.

It's a good thing Jack lets me go, because Sophie and her mom walk in. Dad rushes over to greet them, and Sophie hands me a tray of cupcakes. Each one has my name in blue icing surrounded by a red star.

"Thanks," I say.

"You're welcome." Sophie kisses me on the cheek, like it's no big deal.

Alan Wexler walks in and so does Bubbe's friend Estelle.

Our living room is packed, and even with extra chairs, lots of people are standing. Bubbe carries in trays of food. "Eat, *bube-lahs*, eat."

I think about Mom. I think that she should be here, that she'd love this, but then I realize she wouldn't love it at all. It would make her nervous and scared. She never liked crowds. Hated having to go to parties. She was happiest just being quiet at home. She's happy now. As happy as she can be.

The doorbell rings, and I turn to get it.

"Late as usual," I say, punching Elliott in the arm.

Ms. Berger comes in, too. "Congratulations, sweetie," she says, and kisses my forehead. I wonder if she even knows that Elliott and I weren't friends.

"Party's in here," I say, leading them to the living room.

At eleven, Dad turns on the TV and tells everyone to be quiet. "We don't want to miss this," he says, even though we're recording it.

The moment Jon Stewart appears, the room falls silent. I look over at Elliott, and he gives me a thumbs-up.

Lindsay ruffles my hair.

"Sha!" Bubbe says, even though no one is talking.

After a few jokes about the day's news, Jon Stewart says, "And now, ladies and gentlemen, I want to introduce you to my replacement."

Some people from the TV audience gasp. I hear Sophie squeal, and I get goose bumps on my arms.

"There's a kid in Bensalem, Pennsylvania, who's been making videos for the Internet. His name is David Greenberg."

"Oh, yeah!" Jack says.

"Sha!" Bubbe scolds.

Then Jon Stewart says, "One of the shows was about, um, yours truly. Let's watch it."

And on the screen above Jon's shoulder is the *TalkTime* I did with Magazine Cover Jon Stewart. I cringe at the French horn joke. The clip stops before the Daily Acne Forecast, and I'm so relieved.

Jon says, "Is this guy hilarious or what?"

He's talking about me.

"I definitely think he'll have my job someday." Jon scowls at the camera. "But not yet. And that thing he said about the French horn? Totally true. Totally true. On to other news . . ."

Applause and cheers erupt in our living room. Before I know it, Elliott smashes me on the back, Jack gives me noogies and Lindsay squeezes my hand. "Great job, David. I'm so proud of you," she says.

Bubbe pats my head. "Way to go, *bubelah!*"

Dad grabs me in a killer bear hug.

Even without Mom, I feel completely surrounded by love.

73

The last guest leaves after midnight.

"G'night, guys," Dad says to me and Elliott, who is sleeping over.

"Night, David," Lindsay says.

Bubbe pats my shoulder. "*Oy vey*, I'm tired," she says, and stumbles off to her apartment.

Elliott opens a sleeping bag on the floor near my bed.

When the light's out, he says, "David, you up?"

"Yeah."

"Look, I'm sorry about . . . you know."

"It's okay. Really."

I wait in the dark for Elliott to say something else, but all I hear are soft snoring sounds. I think about Sophie kissing me again and those star cupcakes. I think about all the people watching my video on *The Daily Show*. I think about Elliott sleeping here in my room again, just like old times. And I think about

Mom, who probably wishes she were here, but can't be. It's not her fault, but it's not mine or Dad's or the Farmer's, either.

I turn on the little light over my bed and pull out my Rubik's Cube. I fiddle with it for a while but can't get more than one side the same color. I remember that Mom taught me to close my eyes and visualize myself solving it. I close my eyelids and remember the video I saw with the steps to solving it; then I imagine myself doing each of those steps. I open my eyelids and start doing them. When I get close to the end, I make the last several turns with my eyes closed. When I open them, I'm surprised to see that each side is a solid color.

I wish I could show Mom. I put the cube on my desk so Elliott will see it in the morning. He'll be so impressed.

Then I pull a sheet of paper and a pen from my desk drawer. I think I'm going to write to Mom about the Rubik's Cube, but instead I write this:

Dear Mom,

I'm sorry you couldn't come here, but it's okay. I love you anyway. I will always love you no matter what.

Maybe over Thanksgiving break, Dad will take me to visit you so you won't have to leave your house. If that would be okay.

I'm going to make a new *TalkTime* with Elliott this weekend. And I'll say hello to you on it. And whenever you get a chance to look at it in the library and write a comment, I will read it no matter how many other comments I get.

I love you,

David

I put the letter in an envelope to mail in the morning. Then I listen to the sounds of Elliott's breathing. I think about Lindsay sleeping in the next room and Dad and Bubbe asleep, too. I think about Hammy out in the yard. Maybe I'll get a new hamster someday. Maybe I'll name it Hermy and he'll like being in my videos, too.

I take a deep breath, turn out the light and close my eyes.

Bubbe's Jewish Apple Cake
(If Bubbe isn't available to help with this,
find an adult to assist with slicing and oven work.)

4 large apples
1 tablespoon lemon juice
2 teaspoons cinnamon
4 eggs
1½ cups sugar, plus 2 tablespoons
1 cup applesauce
3 cups flour
3 teaspoons baking powder
½ teaspoon salt
½ cup orange juice
1 tablespoon vanilla
½ cup raisins (optional)
powdered sugar

Preheat oven to 350 degrees F (175 degrees C). Grease and flour a 10-inch tube pan. Pare and slice apples. Soak apples in a large bowl of water with 1 tablespoon lemon juice. Set aside.

Combine two tablespoons sugar and two teaspoons cinnamon and set aside. Beat eggs; beat in 1½ cups sugar gradually; then beat in applesauce. In a separate bowl, combine flour, baking powder and salt. Add flour mixture and orange juice alternately to applesauce mixture, starting with flour mixture, stirring after each addition. Add vanilla and stir. Mix in raisins (optional).

Pour $\frac{1}{4}$ of the batter into greased pan; arrange $\frac{1}{3}$ of the apple slices on top; sprinkle with $\frac{1}{3}$ of the cinnamon mixture. Repeat layers twice, then add a layer of batter to the top.

Bake at 350 degrees for 80 minutes or until a knife comes out clean.

Top with powdered sugar.

Enjoy, *bubelah*!

Glossary of Yiddish Words

bubbe (noun)—grandmother

bubelah (noun)—darling (usually applied to children)

kugel (noun)—a savory or sweet pudding made from noodles or potatoes

matzo (noun)—unleavened bread

matzo ball (noun)—a dumpling made from matzo meal, usually served in soup

mensch (noun)—an honorable, decent person

nashn (verb)—to snack

oy vey! (interjection)—oh, no!; woe is me!

sha! (interjection)—quiet! hush!

sheyn ponem (interjection)—pretty face

schmo (noun)—foolish or stupid person; a goof

vos (pronoun)—what

zeyde (noun)—grandfather

Glossary of Spanish Words

¡Cállate!—Be quiet!
come or *comes* (verb)—eat
computadora (noun)—computer
de nada—you're welcome
escalera (noun)—stairs
gallo (noun)—rooster
gracias—thank you
hámster (noun)—hamster
hija (noun)—daughter
madre (noun)—mother
mesa (noun)—table
mi (pronoun)—my
perro (noun)—dog
puerta (noun)—door
sillas (noun)—chair

About the Author

Donna Gephart's first novel, *As If Being 12¾ Isn't Bad Enough, My Mother Is Running for President!*, won the prestigious Sid Fleischman Humor Award. Donna grew up in Philadelphia and now lives in South Florida with her family. Visit her on the Web at donnagephart.com.